# LOVE HEIST

## Jackie D.

Life Changing Books in conjunction with Power Play Media
Published by Life Changing Books
P.O. Box 423 Brandywine, MD 20613

Library of Congress Cataloging-in-Publication Data;

www.lifechangingbooks.net
13 Digit: 978-1934230732
10 Digit: 1934230731

# Dedication

This book is dedicated to, The Davis Family!

To my son, Emanuel "Poobie" Chapman, I couldn't have asked for a better son. I love you and will always be your biggest fan. To my mother, Janelle Davis, RIP, I miss you dearly. To my dad, Charles "Snoop Bass" Davis, we've been through some rough times, but we as a family came out on top. It's a privilege to be your first born! Everything is everything and everything is…love. To my step mom, Michelle Peebles, thanks for being my mother, friend and a good woman to my dad. To my sister, Michelle Davis, my rock, I don't know where I would be in life if it weren't for you. To my brother, Charlie Davis and his wife, Kat, my nephews, Carlo, Montana and my niece Jasmine.

# Acknowledgements

**To All My BFF's:** Martha Hinton, thanks for being there in some the roughest times of my life. Love you! Tonya Ridley, thirty years strong, thanks for all your help thoughout those years. Sharon Kirkley, please move back to Raleigh, I miss you! Tracey Jones, thanks for always having my back. Frances Pulley, Tonya Pulley and Ciarra Wall, thanks for being there and all the fun we shared traveling up and down the road with our boys. Cynthia Parker, thanks for being a true friend. Barbara Benjamin, I wish you much success with your business, it's remarkable. Kuniki Tabb-Parks, you are a jewel and I wish you and Chris much happiness, shouts out to Nuk, lol  Joy Avery, my friend, consultant and at times therapist, thanks for being there through my stressful times. Carla Williams, almost twenty years strong, I love you and Shamar. Chanda Z., love you girl, five miles to empty. Sandy Satterfield, thanks for some of the best times in my life.

**To My Fam:** To my baby daddy, Big Poobie Chapman and the entire Chapman family in East Orange NJ, I see you Jiles. To my family in the DC/MD area David "Mookie"Washington, Marcus Washington, Shalonda Johnson and family, Arnetta Abney and family, Aunt Lo, Uncle Wayne and to my grandmother Ruth Martin, you are truly missed. To the rest of the Davis family, the Jefferson family and the Peebles family.

**Shouts out to:** Dez, Chris, Melvin, Tevin, Rome, Joel Hardaway aka Bobby James, John Wall, The Great Wall, I told you this day would come. Pam Hubbard, Alvin Massenburg, Nikki Willis, Amity Emerson, The Talk of Town crew, The Vesta crew, Kym Johnson and The Goshawk crew. My son's god father who rarely missed a game since middle school, Stephon "Fat" Lawrence, Box, shouts out to the Raleigh Boys club, Mike Dot sit down somewhere, lol. Tony Edwards, thanks for being in my life and a great role model for my son. To coaches Antone Williams, Travis Davis and Jeff Mavity, thanks for being a part of my son's life and guiding him in the right path. To Rob Man" Williams, thanks for being you, and to your entire family in Durham and Roxboro. To the Garner Rd crew, thanks for starting the path for AAU. Yvonne, Bret and the entire Williams' family, Kizzy Bryant and family, Sandy, Ben and the Blakely Family. Russell Vines, Mikiya Peebles, Chyna Mike, Robbie McNair, thanks for your help on the book, Karen Hodges, Mee Mee, Jamie Mackey, Michelle Peebles, Beefy, Pamela "Pee Wee" Wells, and Jasmine Wilson, thanks for taking the time to read my book early on and encouraging me to keep writing. Amerra Walton, Blanche' Tucker, Dana Brown, Dashiima "Boo" Thompson, Liyah and Mecca Hardy, Robbyn Oak, Jana Yon, Craig "Smooth" Pitts in NJ, Black, Face Diddy. To all my other friends and family that I might have missed, I love you and please forgive me.

**Lastly, Thanks Goes Out To:** To my Life Changing Books family. Azarel, thanks for giving me a chance, (I know you're tired of us! lol) Leslie Allen, you're the bomb girl. Thanks for all your help with this project. Thanks to Nakea Murray, Tasha Simpson, editors and test readers. To Dashawn Taylor, thanks for the hot cover.

**To My Fellow Authors**: Tonya Ridley, Danette Majette, Capone, J. Tremble. Tiphani, Kendall Banks, C. Stecko, Mike Warren, Ericka Williams, Chantel Jolie, Sasha Raye, and anyone else on the LCB crew that I missed…let's get this money.

**A Special Shout Out To**: All the distributors and independent book stores that helped me promote in any way. Lastly, to anyone who purchased Love Heist. I worked hard on this book, so I sincerely appreciate all of your support. Be on the look out for my next one.

Check me out at:
www.facebook.com/loveheist

Peace and Blessings,

*Jackie D.*

# Chapter 1

Russell looked around the dark and gloomy room that had the stench of mold and mildew. He slid to the edge of the twin sized bed and pulled his stiff body to the floor. After doing a long stretch, he slowly moved toward the door. Looking out the narrow rectangular window, Russell was completely in awe when he eyed the small recreation room full of inmates. He then caught a glimpse of a sign above the T.V. that read: *Coleman Federal Correctional Psychiatric Ward, Unit A.* Panicking, Russell scanned the room for someone who worked there, to hopefully get an understanding of what the hell was going on. At that moment, he suddenly became irate and started banging on the locked door.

"Hey, why the fuck did I get moved to the psych ward? I don't belong over here!" he tried to shout. His voice was a bit hoarse. When no one answered him, he began banging again. "Hey, come open this fucking door. I don't belong in here!"

A few seconds later, he noticed a female staff member wearing a white uniform and carrying a small pill tray. When she yelled out, "time for medication," several inmates sitting in the recreation room began to line up against the wall like obedient children.

Russell banged on the door once more to get her attention and this time, the woman finally looked in his direction. But instead of seeing what he wanted, she held up her index finger to let him know it would be a minute. Always known for being impatient, Russell sat down on his bed again, then quickly jumped back up. Pacing the small eight foot wide cell, he tried to recall what happened to land him there, but he couldn't remember. Russell banged his right fist in the palm of his hand before he looked down and noticed all his belongings scattered around on the floor. It was also at that point when he realized he was wearing dingy orange scrubs; a color that wasn't familiar, especially since he was use to his navy blue ones. He stopped dead in his tracks.

"Oh, hell no. Who did this shit?" he yelled out like someone was listening. Russell dropped down on his knees and started picking up the numerous recipes and pictures of different meals that he'd collected over the years. With a strong passion for food and an avid cook, he had plans of opening up a restaurant as soon as he got out of prison. "If anybody in this mutha-fucka touch my shit again, it's gonna be problems. Y'all hear me!"

After stacking his belongings neatly in a pile, he placed them on the small table inside the cell. However, he paid extra special attention to his black and white composition notebook that he almost worshipped. It was a long-term habit for Russell to write certain thoughts down in his notebook along with strange pictures that only made sense in his mind. *How long have I been here*? Russell wondered. He went through his pile again, and pulled out his World's Greatest Chefs calendar, then began to scratch his head. *What the fuck day is it*? Russell scratched his head before he looked at the date April 21st *Russell's Release Date* was scribbled in black ink.

He thought back as far as his memory would take him. April 1st popped in his head. At that moment, it all came back to him. "Oh, shit…the fight." Russell instantly dropped his head into his hands. "I must've really lost it to be up in the psych ward, what the fuck did I do?"

Normally, whenever he got angry, Russell would black out and sometimes draw a complete blank, so now it made sense for him not to remember. However, this time his entire body felt weak. Not to mention, he was nauseated and completely dehydrated. He sat up anxiously, ready to find out the events that led him to be up in this hellhole. After using the bathroom in the filthy toilet, he turned and peeped out the dirty window once again watching the woman impatiently. Suddenly, one guy in particular caught his eye. He was huge, built like a damn line backer. Russell watched as the man slowly walked and lined up with the group to take his medication. He glanced in Russell's direction after taking his meds and headed down the hall like an angry grizzly bear.

"Man, this is some bullshit," Russell said to himself.

Once the nurse finished giving out all the medication a few minutes later, Russell finally saw her walking in his direction. Before entering his room, she grabbed her cell phone off her waist and turned her back to make a call.

Russell liked what he saw. "Damn, baby got a fat ass." He looked her up and down like a fresh piece of meat until she ended her call. She jotted something down on her clipboard, then finally unlocked his door.

"Russell King, I'm Nurse Liyah Graham. I run this Unit. Do you know why you're here?" the woman asked entering the room.

Russell shrugged his shoulders, "No, what the fuck is going on?"

"The paper work here says that you were involved in an altercation with Correctional Officer Douglas in the kitchen."

"Yeah, so what? Muthafuckas fight C.O.'s all the time. They don't end up in this damn ward. Get me the hell up outta here."

Liyah took a step back. As a Psych Nurse, she had to be aware of her surroundings at all times. "Mr. King, don't even think about getting yourself all worked up. Now, you can't be released from this unit until Dr. O'Malley clears you. You're here because after the altercation, you picked up a knife and tried to kill yourself. You were on suicide watch at first, but after we couldn't calm you down, unfortunately we had to give you a sedative. You've only been in this ward overnight, but it may seem longer to you."

"Yeah, it feels like a damn year."

Liyah looked down at the clipboard again. "Now, are you able to recollect what happened?"

Russell shook his head. "I can't remember all of it, but I do remember that after all these years of trying, I finally got a job working in the kitchen. You know I love to cook and be around food."

"I'm sure you do," Liyah said unenthused. After only four years at the prison, she was already tired of the inmates and their stories.

"Well, that red neck muthafucka C.O. Douglas was assigned to the kitchen and dining hall. His ass fucked with me from the first day I started. Instead of doing his job, he expected every inmate in the kitchen to bow down and kiss his ass. He came in the kitchen that day and threw a pan of food on the floor and tried to make me clean the shit up. When I refused, he hit me with another pan and pushed me down on the floor. Then I think he yelled something like "get it up with your mouth nigga boy," if I can remember correctly. I mean shit…I know Florida is considered the south, but we ain't in damn Mississippi. After that, I obviously flipped the fuck out. I don't even think he had time to call for backup."

"Well, Mr. King I'm afraid you did more than that." Liyah read from the paper on the clipboard, then looked up. "According to this, you beat him severely, and even broke his arm. After which, you grabbed a knife and put it to your throat. Once the C.O.'s were finally able to get the knife away, you suffered some type of break down and then went into shock."

"Man, these muthafucking C.O.'s probably lying on me. See, that's what they do around here," Russell interrupted.

Liyah read from the paper again. "It says here that while

the Correction Officers were escorting you to this ward, you were mumbling some crazy things, especially about your mother."

"Man, fuck that bitch. Don't even bring her up. Ever!" Russell began shaking his leg. At that moment, he grabbed his notebook and wrote the words, I HATE HER in all capital letters.

Liyah wondered if she should've gotten a few of the C.O.'s to escort her into the cell. Even though she was allowed to carry a small emergency can of mace in her pocket, for some reason it didn't seem like it would work on Russell, especially with his solid, muscular build. "Mr. King whenever something like this happens, the inmate is sent to this unit to be evaluated, and again in your case put under suicide watch. Now, here we are." She tried to force a smile, hoping it would calm him down. "Mr. King, I just called and informed Dr. O'Malley about your progress. You have an appointment to meet her in the morning."

"Man, I can't believe this. What about that red neck? Does he still work here?"

"C.O. Douglas has been put on administrative leave. He was already under investigation. A lot of the inmates came to your defense. Word around the facility is that he may be released from his position."

"Hold up, wait a damn minute. Is this shit gonna affect me from getting out?" Russell began to think about the parole hearing he'd just had a month ago. After serving sixteen years on an eighteen year bid in Florida, he was finally getting out. A decision that had been made with the help of the doctor's recommendations. "Dr. O'Malley said I was doing great. She even took me off the Lithium right before my parole hearing." Russell wasn't a stranger to the prison's only psychiatrist, especially since he'd been diagnosed with paranoid schizophrenia. Although, he had ongoing evaluations, he'd never been admitted to the psych ward.

*They obviously need to put your ass back on that shit,* Liyah thought. "I'm not sure Mr. King. I guess it is possible for the parole board to overturn their decision."

All Russell could do was shake his head. He prayed that this incident wasn't going to mess up his chances of finally getting out.

"Okay, Mr. King, listen up. You've been assigned to my Unit. It's an open unit, which means there's minimum observation over here. We try to make life as normal as possible. However, cell doors are locked unless its time for recreation, doctor evaluations or other activities."

Russell rubbed his stomach in a circular motion. "What about food? I'm hungry as hell."

"Oh, yes I forgot about meals." Liyah looked at her watch. "You found a bad time to snap out of it because you just missed dinner, actually. I'll see if I can find you something to hold you until breakfast. However, let me say this. I don't want any shit from you. If you follow the rules, you will remain in my unit. If not, I will ship your ass up outta here as fast as you came in. There are two psych wards, Unit A and B. This is unit A. Trust me, you don't want to be in the other unit. Do you understand?" Liyah held a stern look on her face. Something she'd been trained to do when she first started. Along with the rule, never befriend an inmate.

Russell responded by nodding his head, letting her know he understood. He was glad she had finally shut up. He then suddenly began sizing her up again. *She trying to talk all professional, but that bitch got hood rat written all over her; she's probably about twenty-five with about four kids,* he thought.

He was usually on point when it came to reading a woman. She was a cutie pie, tall and thick like Tyra Banks and a big, plump, round ass that only a woman who got her work out on would have. The only flaw he could find other than she talked too much was her jacked up weave that showed she was long overdue for a visit to the salon. Russell liked a woman to keep her hair, nails and toes done on a regular basis. Growing up around his cousin, Portia, who was the flyest chick he knew, it made his standards really high. He often compared women to her whenever it was necessary. Only one year apart in age, he and Portia were inseparable and often never seen apart when they were growing up.

"You only have about an hour before lights out so let's go. I know you probably wanna get out of this room for a minute," Liyah said, backing up. Another important rule was to never turn her back on an inmate.

Russell didn't hesitate following the nurse into the recreation room. As he looked around, he realized that the psych ward was a different world compared to his previous cell block. With it's foul order, and peeling eggshell colored paint, it looked dirty and depressing. He even wondered where the nearest padded room was. He watched as some inmates rocked back and forth in their seats while others stared into thin air or yelled out obscenities.

"So, what the fuck am I supposed to do out here?" he asked.

"You can do whatever you want. Watch T.V., read, act crazy, it's all up to you. Just don't get too out of hand. I'ma go and try to get you something to eat." Putting the clipboard under her arm, Liyah walked away leaving Russell standing there.

"Man, I can't believe I'm in this place," he mumbled to himself. "And I'ma let Dr. O'Malley know that shit, too." Russell walked around the area for a minute, before finding a chair that was a good distance away from the other inmates.

After Liyah brought him back two bags of potato chips, an apple, and a bottle of water, Russell sat in the same spot the entire time not saying a word to anyone. Instead, he constantly observed his surroundings. Every now and then he would glance over at the T.V. at some old black and white movie that seemed to play over and over. That is until a fight between two inmates suddenly broke out over a game of dominoes. The two men fought, knocking over tables and chairs until blood appeared. When four guards came and broke it up, two of them had to pry a homemade shank from the hands of one of the men. While being led away from the scene, he constantly threw up his fingers that appeared to be gang signs, but no one was sure. Meanwhile, the other man, who was stabbed in the face, constantly screamed out "The devil is trying to kill me!" It was a disturbing scene.

"Shit, I thought my old cell block was full of crazy niggas, but this place is a fucking nut house," Russell said.

Maybe from all the violence, visions of Russell's wife flashed in front of him, he closed his eyes to try and block out the night he argued with her and pushed her down the stairs to her death. He remembered the night like it was yesterday; the night she stood with her bags packed telling him she was leaving him for another man. Obviously fed up with Russell's mood swings, neglect and verbal abuse, she was ready to move on. Seeing his wife of only six months with two suitcases, instantly reminded him of his mother, who not only physically abused him as a child, but had the nerve to walk out on his life at the age of fifteen. A woman who'd been on drugs most of her life and terrorized him constantly. Not only did she let him down, but she let Portia down as well. With Portia's mother dying in a car accident when she was only five, his mother was supposed to be her legal guardian and caretaker, but she never fit that bill. She used the monthly checks Portia received from her mother's death on drugs, alcohol or the countless men in her life.

In a fit of rage, Russell walked up and punched his wife repeatedly until she somehow got away. He caught up with her at the staircase and didn't even hesitate before giving her a forceful push. The sound of her head hitting two steps on the way down was confirmation that she was dead...instantly. Russell's nosey neighbors ended up calling the police. When they got there, he was sitting in the bathtub burning all her pictures. He'd also written the words, "Fuck the world" all over the wall in his own blood. It was definitely some Charles Manson type of shit.

Russell had plans to plead temporary insanity, but his lawyer convinced him to cop to a second degree murder charge instead. The prosecutor didn't have much evidence to get a first degree conviction anyway. There were no real motives for his actions especially since no one knew they were married anyway.

When Russell finally opened his eyes and saw Liyah watching him, he knew before long he would have her eating out the palm of his hands. Since his stay in prison, he had all the female guards fighting over him and she was no exception. Although, he often treated women like shit, Russell had a gift. His talk game and big dick was on point.

Moments later, Russell looked up when he heard a voice come over the loud speaker. "All inmates. Please report to your cells. Lights out."

When Russell looked at the clock on the wall and realized it was only 9:00 p.m., he became frustrated. "Shit, you got to be kidding me. We could stay up 'til 11:00 in my old cell block," he said, watching the inmates drag themselves to their rooms. Most seemed to be completely drugged up from the medication.

"I gotta hold myself together long enough to see the doctor in the morning," Russell told himself as he stared at the ceiling in disbelief that he was even actually there in the first place.

"Okay, Russell King, don't make this difficult, let's go!" Liyah yelled.

Not putting up a fight, Russell got up and walked back to his room and laid down. Once all the lights were turned off, he closed his eyes and tried to relax, but found it extremely difficult; especially since he could hear some of the other inmates yelling. He tried to imagine he was somewhere else. When that didn't work, he tossed and turned on the hard bed, unable to sleep as beads of sweat dripped off his muscular body.

"Damn, it's hot as fish grease in this muthafucka." The only advantage of being in the crazy ward was that he finally had a cell to himself.

Not being able to take the heat, he stripped down butt naked. He missed being able to sleep nude. Something he enjoyed and did on a regular when he was a free man. Russell then placed his hands on his dick, slowly moving it around, then up and down and in a circular motion. He started jacking his dick faster as he rubbed and pulled at his balls with the other hand. Jerking off was another activity he enjoyed.

He moaned out loud as he pictured himself in bed with a bad bitch. Thinking about a nice tight pussy, he forcefully continued pumping his dick. After a few loud grunts, cum began to shoot out like a water fountain. The release felt good. He laid there a minute, still in a daze. Moments later, Russell reached over and wiped his self off with the stiff white sheets before noticing what looked like a shadow outside his cell door. Somebody was watching him.

"If one of you crazy muthafuckas is peeping at me, I got something for that ass. I don't play that gay shit, for real!" Russell yelled lifting his head up.

When he heard some shuffling noises and then footsteps walking away, he laid his head back on the bed grabbed his dick and started stroking it again, this time much harder. That is until he heard noises outside his door again. Russell was pissed off wondering who could've been watching him. He quickly jumped up and ran toward the window in hopes of catching the Peeping Tom this time. However, once he looked out, no one was there. If that wasn't bad enough, when Russell turned back around, he instantly felt an anxiety attack coming on when he saw his dead wife sitting on the edge of his bed.

He closed his eyes for a few seconds then opened them back up, but his wife was still there.

"Get the hell out of here!"

"Russell you killed me, why did you kill me?"

"You shouldn't have tried to leave me for another nigga!" Russell shot back.

"I loved you Russell!" the voice in his head said.

"Whatever, you're just like my mother. She was supposed to love me, too. Leave me alone bitch!"

# Chapter 2

Lyric, Portia and Sheena cruised around uptown Charlotte, NC in a pink super- stretch Hummer H2; a specialty limo that Lyric rented for this special occasion. The streets were jumping with bumper to bumper cars on both sides as crowds of people stood on the sidewalks socializing. Lyric smiled as she watched the women prancing around from car to car half dressed in their hoochie dresses looking for a come up.

"Damn, I didn't know uptown Charlotte was doing it like this. I've' been cooped up in the suburbs way too long," Lyric said. She would've swore she was on The Las Vegas Strip as the systems thumped and the ballers cruised up and down the crowded street determined to show off their rimmed up whips. The only thing missing were the bright lights, The MGM Grand, and Caesar's Palace.

Heads turned in curiosity as people peered to see who was in the bubble gum colored vehicle as it slowly passed. At that moment, Sheena jumped up out of her seat, dropping the empty bottle of Rose Moet on the floor. She went straight for the open rooftop.

"The world is mine!" she screamed while her weave

blew violently in the wind.

"Sheena, sit your ghetto-ass down! Don't nobody want to look at your nasty-ass thongs," Portia joked while having no choice but to look up her childhood friend's dress.
"And stop yelling all that dumb Al Pacino shit. We can't take your ass anywhere."

Lyric agreed with a huge laugh.

Sheena plopped back down in her seat and rolled her eyes before fixing her expensive Malaysian weave. "Shit, some-body need to set the night off right. Y'all bitches wanna ride around like its prom night or some shit, tryna look all prim and proper. Fuck that, Portia, you need to get your ass up and start celebrating. You getting married in two weeks. I'm ready to have some damn fun, and get my sexy on!"

Sheena took it a bit further and spread her legs as she hit the floor doing a cheerleader type split. Lyric and Portia both looked at each other wondering what went wrong in their friend's life to make her act the way she did. Sheena was an at-tractive honey-coated woman, 5'5, small waist and a huge ass that drove men crazy just like the model, Rosa Acosta. Sheena wore a short black skin tight, v-neckline Prada dress exposing her perky 36 double D's. This wasn't out of the ordinary for her, she loved attention. Her skimpy outfits and slutty demeanor made most men know right out the gate she was a loose woman. As one of the top strippers at Club Onyx, damn near every man around town knew her by name. A certified freak and proud of it.

Sheena admitted on the regular, she loved sex anywhere and with anybody; whether it be a hard dick or a wet clit, she was down. As much as her friends disliked her lifestyle, they knew Sheena was going to be herself regardless of what they said. So, to avoid having to argue with her all night, they fell back and let her do her thing.

After watching Sheena flaunt and flirt with the limo driver for a few minutes, Portia knew exactly what to say to calm her ass down.

"Sheena, did I tell you my cousin, Russell is getting out of jail soon, and might be coming to the wedding?" I can't wait to see him, I miss him. It was fucked up what happened. He never should've gone to prison in the first damn place. That shit with his  wife falling was an accident."

"I miss Russ, too." Lyric agreed. "Hell, I didn't even know Russell had a wife when you first told me that story."

Portia shook her head. "Shit, me either. I didn't know until a month after he went to prison. You know he changed women like he changed his underwear, so I couldn't keep up."

"That's because he couldn't keep any," Lyric joked.

Sheena paused and looked off into space before speaking. "I don't give a shit about Russell, Portia. Was that comment supposed to mean something to me? Fuck that crazy-ass nigga. Don't mention his name to me again!" Her mood had changed instantly.

Portia watched Sheena's face frown as she grabbed another bottle of Moet from the wet bar, popped the top, then turned it up. She knew Sheena used to be crazy in love with Russell back in the day, but her reaction was more intense than she expected.

Lyric reached in her new Chanel purse, grabbed her diamond covered Blackberry phone and called her man, Diesel. She'd been calling all day, but he had yet to answer her call. After a few rings, she listened as he said hello with an attitude.

"Why didn't you come home last night, Diesel?" Lyric whispered into the phone.

He sighed. "Cause I didn't feel like it, and I knew you would be actin' like a damn mosquito, naggin' the fuck out of me. Aren't you out with your friends anyway? Why you worried about what the fuck I'm doing?" His disrespectful ways were nothing new. Over the past two years, he'd been treating Lyric like shit, causing their relationship to be completely unhealthy.

"What up, Ma?" he asked in his thick New York accent.

"Where were you, Diesel? You could've at least called and told me you weren't coming home." Lyric said, still whispering in her phone. "So, where are you now?"

"Yo, Lyric, stop drillin' me. Have a good time in New York. I gave yo' ass $5,000 so you and yo' girls could ball outta control. That's all you should be concerned about," Diesel replied. "Any other bitch would love to get that type of dough."

Lyric hated when Diesel constantly threw comments in her face about what other woman would be grateful to have from him. She also never got a chance to tell him that she and her friends had decided at the last minute not to fly to New York for the weekend. "If you would've answered your phone earlier I could've told you that…"

Diesel cut her off. "Look, I gotta go."

She could feel her girls looking at her sideways for calling him in the first place. She definitely didn't want them to hear her arguing with Diesel yet again. So she played it off. "Alright, baby. Call me as soon as you get a minute. I'll make sure I keep my phone in my hand."

"Don't worry, I wont be callin'. I'll be out of town by the time you get back. I'll holla at you then," Diesel said coldly.

"Where are you going? When are you coming back?" This was the same conversation, just a different day.

"Lyric, you really makin' my damn head hurt wit' all this shit. Like I said…I'll see yo' ass when I get back." CLICK

"Bye baby," Lyric said, pretending to end her call. She was mad as hell that she couldn't curse him out like she really wanted to.

Portia cut her eye in Lyric's direction, after seeing her facial expression she knew all that, *okay baby shit* during the conversation with Diesel was a front. She hadn't heard Lyric and Diesel talk like that in almost two years. "You really need to leave him."

Lyric turned her head and looked out the dark tinted window. "It's not as easy as you think."

"No, she shouldn't. That nigga be hooking her ass up. Plus, we benefit from that shit," Sheena added.

"It's true, Portia. Diesel always finances whatever we

want to do," Lyric admitted.

Portia shook her head. "You can't continue to be with a man, just for his money. So what, you wanna die paid, but unhappy. He doesn't even want kids with you."

Lyric lowered her head thinking about the lie she'd told her friends. The truth was, with her contracting Chlamydia from Diesel twice, and not detecting it in time, the disease had spread to her fallopian tubes leaving her infertile. Lyric's heart ached every time she thought about it.

"Don't sacrifice your well-being for someone who doesn't appreciate you," Portia continued. "The fact that he doesn't respect you just proves that you deserve much more."

"Oh, my God. Bitch, will you shut up with that Oprah shit?" Sheena shot back. "That nigga Diesel paid, which makes him just fine."

Lyric lowered her head and played with her phone like she was in deep thought.

In hopes to cheer her best friend up, Portia clapped her hands. "Alright…that's it, phones off. No more calling your "man", because it's my bachelorette party tonight and we're about to have a night to remember!"

"Bout fucking time!" Sheena yelled pissy drunk as she grabbed another bottle.

Portia turned to Lyric and smiled. "You with us?"

Not wanting to ruin her friend's night, Lyric returned the smile. "Of course."

As the driver turned on East Stonewall Street, the girls toasted their glasses while singing along with Shawty Lo's video, *Dey Know* as it played on the forty-two-inch custom LCD T.V. screen inside the limo. While sipping the champagne, Lyric sat back and tried to relax on the comfortable pink and white two-toned leather seats. Looking around, she admired the state of the art audio system, and the custom lighting that ran the entire length of the vehicle. Portia had seen the limo online, and since pink was her favorite color, Lyric felt honored to rent it for her friend. She'd also rented a penthouse suite at a luxury four diamond hotel for the second part of the night.

Lyric looked up through the sunroof noticing the full moon that lingered above thinking about how Portia has always been there for her. Lyric didn't want to disappoint her best friend, who was just like her sister. Portia and her grandmother, Mama Moses who'd passed away from cancer several years ago had taken her in when she was just fourteen years old and left homeless by her drug addicted mother.

"Damn, that's a fine piece of chocolate standing right there in front of the club. He looks almost as good as my husband, Morris Chestnut." Sheena moved closer to the back window and rolled it down to try and get his attention. "Hey, boo!" Sheena yelled out in a drunken rant with half her body hanging out.

Lyric glanced out the window at the man Sheena was referring to. "Damn, he is fine," Lyric said to herself. Seconds later, her spirits were dampened, when she spotted a familiar face amongst the crowd.

"Oh shit, stop the car now!" Lyric yelled to the driver. "I know that ain't Diesel, that lying bastard! I know his car anywhere."

When the truck came to a stop, Lyric jumped out looking like a true movie star in a beige snakeskin Alexander McQueen dress, and a pair of banging peep toe Christian Louboutin ankle boots that matched her dress perfectly. Lyric resembled Keyshia Cole and was mistaken for her on a regular basis. Her long, jet black wavy hair was full of body and flowed down her back. She also had the cutest dimples, but you could barely see them with the frown that was now formed on her beautiful face. She'd known all her life that her father was white, but since her mother was a crack head, her father could've been anybody.

"Shit, here...we...go again," Sheena said, pulling off her earrings and snatching her weave back into a pony tail. "Lets get...ready to r-u-m-b-l-e." She stumbled over every other word she managed to get out, but made sure she put emphasis on the last one.

As Diesel pulled up to valet parking, Lyric could see the silhouette of a female in the passenger seat of his black Maserati GranTurismo fixing her hair. At that moment, she also glanced over and noticed a dark colored GS 430 Lexus with tinted windows a few cars behind him. She thought back, *is that the same Lexus I saw behind me a few days ago?* "Naww," she said, brushing it off.

When Lyric looked back toward the club, she completely lost it this time when she saw the woman clinging to the arm of Diesel's Dolce & Gabbana jacket, looking needy, yet confident at the same time as if he was her man. They walked inside Club Ice like a certified couple.

Portia quickly jumped out the limo and ran behind Lyric. "Wait, pump your brakes," Portia said, stepping in front of her friend. "Not only have you been pouting ever since you got off the phone with Diesel, and trying to play it off, but I know that look. You about to fight another girl who probably doesn't even know you exist."

Sheena stumbled up behind them and pointed. "So what? Let's go get her ass!"

Portia ignored her. "Look, Lyric every time we go out it's the same shit. This is supposed to be my night, all about me, remember? I'm the one getting married, but once again Diesel has managed to spoil another one of our nights out. When is enough gonna be enough?"

"Never!" Sheena yelled as she butted into their conversation. "As long as Diesel, the big time drug dealer continues to take care of her ass, giving her stacks of money to spend and she living up in that fly ass crib with him, she will continue to let him treat her like shit and fight over his ass! And you and I will continue to help her ass fight, because she's our girl and we roll like that!" Sheena said, dancing around to the music blaring from a nearby car.

"Shut up with your drunk-ass!" Portia fired back.

"No, you shut up, Portia." Sheena stepped up in her friend's face. "Ever since you agreed to marry that uppity nigga, you've changed. Always giving us lectures and shit. We don't wanna hear that all the time. Stop being all booshie!"

"We should all be changing. We're thirty-four, but acting like damn teenagers!" Portia fired back.

"Whatever. I don't even know why you with his ass anyway. You already said he couldn't fuck," Sheena informed.

"Do you have to keep saying that shit? It's more to a relationship than sex," Portia lied. In actuality, she hated the fact that Charles was so bad in bed.

"Whatever. Ain't nothing better than a man with a big stiff dick who knows how to work the middle."

Lyric paused briefly ignoring Sheena, but looking Portia in her chinky shaped eyes. She looked as if she had a Korean heritage, but was actually straight from the old Piedmont Courts projects. Portia stood 5'7' with natural, chin length black hair that she wore with a low bang. She wasn't a weave queen like Sheena, but did add a few pieces here and there to give herself different looks. She also wasn't into high end designers like her friends. If she was able to find a cute shirt from her favorite store, Express or even Target, that suited her just fine. All she seemed to be into lately anyway was her man.

Lyric knew Portia was right, but all she had on her mind was Diesel and that bitch that he paraded like a trophy. She took off toward the club, breathing out of control. She stopped in her tracks when she saw Diesel's car sitting in the valet parking a few yards away.

Not thinking twice, she quickly walked over to the hundred thousand dollar car, with Sheena right behind her. She knew what Lyric was about to do and wanted to help. Portia on the other hand stayed back.

"Hurry up, Lyric," Portia said, acting as look-out. She didn't agree with her friend's decision, but wasn't about to let her go down.

Lyric reached in her bag and pulled out her razor then scratched the hood, the driver's side, and then slit two tires. Sheena was about to grab the razor to do the other tires, when

Lyric noticed Portia waving her hands in the air.

"Oh, shit, that's Diesel's car. The nigga I was telling you about who got all that paper," a dude said.

"Let's go, somebody's watching us," Lyric informed.

"Code ten," Sheena replied imitating Keyshia Cole's mother, Frankie. She quickly walked away.

"Let's see how good your ass look with your shit all scratched up," Lyric said, as if Diesel was listening.

# LOVE HEIST

# Chapter 3

When Lyric reached the front door of the club she looked over her shoulder toward her girls to see if they had her back or if she was flying solo. Like always, they were two steps behind and ready for whatever.

"Oh hell no, I don't do lines," Lyric said, noticing several girls with short dresses shivering. Even though it was spring, the weather at night was still fairly chilly. Not to mention, she was use to getting VIP status by being Diesel's girl.

When she recognized the bouncer who always let her and Diesel in at the door, Lyric told her girls, "We good, come on." However, when they approached him he quickly pointed his thick index finger in the opposite direction.

"Ladies, the line is over there."

"So, you trying to act like you don't remember me? As much as I come up in this damn club with my man, Diesel!" Lyric shouted.

"Look, baby girl, I'm just doing my job," the bouncer replied without giving her much eye contact.

Lyric thought maybe he was on Diesel's payroll. She looked at the heavy-set bouncer, reached in her purse and bent over like she'd dropped something to get his full attention. She then licked her lips and batted her long fake eye lashes all the while slipping him a hundred-dollar bill.

After a quick glance at Benjamin Franklin, he studied her body up and down with lust filled eyes before speaking. "Yo sexy, make sure you bring me that phone number before the night is out, I don't care who your man is," he said, lifting the red rope so they could pass through.

"Okay, Big Daddy," Lyric replied, playing the role.

They all laughed at his sloppy-ass knowing he didn't stand a chance. Once inside, Lyric looked down on the huge dance floor full of people and couldn't believe how packed it was. The club had to be over capacity. Lyric loved the clubs top of the line ice inspired interior, eleven flat screens and five bars. She enjoyed anything upscale. Another reason why she loved the club so much was because she'd been kicked out of all the other black clubs for fighting. Fortunately for her, she'd never been locked up for it.

Heads turned as the three cuties maneuvered through the crowd.

"This spot is popping tonight!" Sheena yelled over the loud music shaking her ass with every step. After about ten minutes of scanning the cram-packed club Lyric saw the sign that read, VIP Lounge.

"I know that's where Diesel is," Lyric said to Portia as she headed straight in that direction.

"Go with me to the bathroom first," Portia said.

Lyric frowned. "Are you serious? Now?"

"Yes, now." Portia grabbed both Lyric's and Sheena's arms and pulled them inside the bathroom.

She didn't even care that the room was full of women before she began to lecture...again. "Lyric, just let Diesel's ass know that you've seen him and then leave. It hurts niggas worst when you act like shit don't bother you. All that fighting is getting old. It's time to put that razor up and act like a lady for once. Shit, the way all these dudes digging you tonight, Diesel can quickly be replaced," Portia said, hoping she was able to get through to her friend.

*Yeah, but I doubt if they can replace his paper*, Lyric thought. "Portia, I hear you, but I'm just so sick of his ass. I'm so mad right now that I wanna turn this damn club out!"

"Man, don't listen to Portia. Get his ass Lyric; he must've forgotten who he dealin' with," Sheena said egging her on.

Several women in the bathroom snickered.

"Lyric, have I ever steered you wrong?" Portia pleaded.

Lyric shook her head. "No."

"Then handle this shit correctly," Portia replied. "Besides, I can't be seen fighting in the clubs anymore. Charles would kill me. He has a reputation to uphold. Hell, Charles doesn't even know what Diesel does for a living. I lied and told him that Diesel buys and sells properties." Thinking about her fiancé, Portia looked down and eyed her two carat princess cut ring. There was no way she was about to risk her upcoming nuptials.

"Then leave," Sheena suggested.

"I love you, Portia, but fuck that!" Lyric said, as she proceeded out the door and toward VIP.

"Yeah, fuck that," Sheena repeated. She was on Lyric's heels in no time, with Portia not far behind.

The guy working the VIP entrance was so busy flirting with a girl off to the side, he never noticed Lyric and her crew as they stepped right inside like they belonged. It was a totally different atmosphere than the rest of the loud crowded club. With at least three bottles of champagne and the sparkling liqueur, Nuvo on each table, everyone in attendance looked like they had money. It didn't take long before Lyric noticed Diesel in the corner of the room with his back turned. He was engaged in a conversation with some of his boys along with the female's arm draped intimately around his slim waist. Rage took over as Lyric headed in that direction unzipping her purse and quickly slid out her razor again. The expression that appeared on one of the dude's face when he saw Lyric rushing toward them made Diesel turn around instantly.

"Damn, here comes the bullshit," Diesel said, knowing he'd been busted...again.

The women looked up as Lyric headed her way. She was confused by all the commotion. "Who's that, Diesel?" she asked nervously.

"Our worst nightmare." He removed her arm and backed away, putting as much distance between them as he could, then rubbed his bald head.

When Lyric walked up on Diesel, who appeared to be sweating bullets, something quickly came over her. At that moment, she heard Portia's voice in her head causing her to switch to an entirely different mind frame. She quickly dropped the razor back in her purse.

"Hey, Diesel baby, you decided to stay in town, I see," Lyric said, kissing him on the lips. She turned to the direction of the slim, chocolate colored chick, who had a choppy haircut like the R&B singer, Monica and the beauty of a super model.

Lyric extended her hand. "Hello, I'm Diesel's fiancé; I hope you're enjoying yourself tonight." When a female waitress walked up, Lyric quickly got her attention. "Waiter, can you bring the lady a bottle of Cristal on me? Actually, you can go ahead and pour a few glasses as well." Lyric turned back toward the woman and smiled. This time her dimples could be easily seen. "It was nice to meet you sweetie. Please excuse me, I'm on my way to hit the town and celebrate with my girls." She then looked at Diesel. "See you at home, baby. Oh, and you need to make sure you take your penicillin. The doctor called today to confirm that you have another STD, Gonorrhea to be exact!" Lyric said, walking away and winking her eye at Diesel.

Both the female and Diesel stood speechless. A few seconds later, Diesel glanced at Lyric who turned and looked back in his direction. When their eyes met, Lyric saw the puzzled look on his face.

"C'mon girl," Portia said laughing. She grabbed Lyric by the arm again, dragging her out of VIP. "Fuck Mr. String Bean." Portia often called Diesel that because he was so skinny."

Sheena however looked disappointed. "That was some bullshit. I thought you were gonna slice her ass up. I need somethin' else to drink now. That stunt you just pulled blew my damn high!"

"Did you see how stupid he looked standing there? He's so use to Lyric always fighting over his ass and causing a scene, he doesn't know how to take her now," Portia pointed out.

"Yeah, you were right. I'm tired of fighting over someone who's obviously not worth it. I've cut so many bitches that I lost count. I'm fed up." At that moment, Lyric had it in her mind that messing up his car was no longer good enough. The car could easily be repainted, and the tires replaced. This time, Lyric wanted him to feel some of the pain she constantly had to endure. "Let's get out of here."

"Damn, can I at least get a drink?" Sheena questioned.

"No, I'm ready to go. There's more champagne in the limo," Lyric stated.

They all headed out the door and were immediately distracted by the loud roaring sounds of motorcycles pulling up. They watched as a female bike club lined their motorcycles up one by one along the curb kicking out the stands with their fashionable boots. They all had on red jackets with their club logo, *The Diva Stars* written across the shoulders. It looked like something off a movie set.

"Now, that's what the fuck I'm talkin' 'bout," Sheena said, losing her mind. She eyed all the female bikers like her favorite food.

When they started taking off their helmets, Lyric stopped walking and did a double take when she thought she recognized her older cousin, Kendra, who she hadn't seen in years. She watched as the female placed her helmet on her seat, fixed her long thick dreads, then pulled up her black jeans before glancing in her direction.

"Lyric, is that you?" she asked, with a surprised look.

"Kendra?" Lyric asked, walking over to hug her.

Kendra had been in and out of prison most of Lyric's life,

which was devastating, especially since Kendra was the only person in Lyric's family who cared about her. The last time she went on a mandatory vacation was four years ago on an aggravated assault charge against her girlfriend. Just like all the other prison stays, Lyric wrote Kendra almost every day, but somehow when she moved in with Diesel, they somehow lost contact with each other.

"What up cuz?" Kendra replied. "Damn, I been searching for your ass ever since I got out." The girls hugged each other for a few minutes before releasing their grip.

"Look at you. Your ass all iced out, looking like money. You hitting some nigga in the head big time I see," Kendra said, with a huge grin. She remembered how hard Lyric had it growing up, and was glad to see that her little cousin had turned out alright.

"I know. Shit, it looks like you put on some weight," Lyric noticed. "Damn, did you get taller, too?" Her cousin's 5'9' height seemed to loom over her 5'4' frame.

Kendra smiled. "Yeah, a bitch wear about a fourteen now. Shit, maybe more than that. These jeans kinda tight, now that I think about it."

Kendra turned and introduced Lyric to her biker club. "Yo, this is my baby cuz, Lyric. I used to baby sit this bitch and let her wear all my clothes cause she didn't have none. Now, look at her ass!" The biker club all laughed.

Lyric spoke to the women and then suddenly walked away. She didn't like being reminded of her childhood or the fact that she was so poor. Still to this day, she didn't like to be the butt of anyone's joke.

Kendra walked behind her. "So, who you rolling with tonight? I hope you not out here by yourself?"

Lyric came out her daze. "I'm with Portia and Sheena. You remember them, don't you?" she asked, as the Hummer pulled up. Sheena was a few feet away surrounded by a group of females, but still managed to wave at Kendra like an innocent schoolgirl. There was an instant attraction.

"Hell yeah I remember them." Kendra hugged Portia then looked back at Lyric. "I just don't remember Sheena being that thick. Damn, I need to be rolling with y'all tonight, nice Hummer," Kendra said, eyeballing Sheena up and down.

Lyric chose not to entertain that statement. "So, where are you staying?"

"Over in the Sugar Creek area. I got a fly loft apartment. You need to come check me out."

"Shit, not on that bad side of town." Lyric mumbled remembering the day she almost got robbed in that area.

"Bitch don't act like you was born with a silver spoon in your mouth," Kendra replied. "As a matter of fact I need to holla at you for a minute." The two of them walked away from the crowd. "I hate to ask you this, but you got a couple of dollars your cuz can hold? That bullshit job I got doesn't pay anything, but until I'm off parole, I have to continue to work there."

Lyric remembered how she would've gone hungry plenty of nights if Kendra hadn't come around to bring her food when she was younger, so returning the favor now wasn't a problem. She wasn't even going to ask Kendra how she could afford to get a bike without any money. She reached inside her purse and peeled off three hundred dollars and passed it to her cousin.

"Thanks Lyric, take my number so we can hang out," Kendra suggested as the cousins exchanged phone numbers.

Kendra turned around to watch Sheena walking up toward them. "Is your cousin coming along with us to the party tonight, Lyric?" Sheena asked. She licked her lips like LL Cool J.

"No, she isn't Sheena! Talk to you later, cuz." Lyric knew why she was asking and it wasn't going down if she could help it.

"What party?" Kendra asked.

"It's round two of Portia's bachlorette party. She's getting married," Lyric informed.

"Lyric, I just saw some of my friends coming out the club. They want to ride in the limo to the hotel, is that gonna be problem? Portia already said it was cool," Sheena informed her.

"I have too many problems to care about minor shit like that now," Lyric said, walking off. "I'll talk to you later, cuz. Let's go, Sheena."

Little did she know, Kendra wasn't about to let Sheena leave without getting her phone number or whatever else Sheena was willing to give. They talked and giggled for a minute while Lyric and Portia climbed into the limo.

Once everyone, including Sheena's entourage of about fifteen females were all inside truck, Lyric peeped out the window when she realized Sheena still hadn't gotten in. She watched as Kendra walked off and got on her bike. A few seconds later, Sheena ran over and got on the back of the bike with her. "That shit is ridiculous."

"We'll never be able to understand Sheena, so just let it go," Portia advised.

"Yeah, I guess you're right. Driver, let's get up outta here. Roll over top of these damn cars if you have to." When they got about a block away Lyric instructed, "To the Hilton on East Third Street."

During the ride, Lyric was silent while the rest of the girls in the stretch partied. She wasn't feeling the whole Sheena and Kendra situation. "The shit is not gonna be good," Lyric said to herself. She rolled down the window and poked her head out, watching the two of them riding behind on a red and black Honda CBR. She shook her head again. *I wonder if Kendra has changed,* Lyric wondered. She felt the need to warn Sheena about her cousin, but didn't want to be labeled a hater. *Maybe I'm just overreacting.* Until things got out of hand, Lyric decided to just stay in her lane.

Moments later, she went into her own little world recalling the events of the night. In her mind, she visualized the old Lyric, and how she would've normally wiped the floor with that girl's ass without even blinking, but the thought of it all, painted a negative image in her head letting Lyric know she was slowly changing. She breathed deeply as she stared out the window asking herself, why she kept putting up with Diesel and his cheating? *As many times as I have caught him cheating on me, I still hang around. All because I love him, and I love the way he provides for me even more.*

Lyric remembered the dirty one bedroom roach infested apartment she lived in with her crack addicted mother. Her mother sold her body to support her habit, and always left Lyric alone to fend for herself at an early age. She learned to survive by stealing, whether it was out of her mother's many sexual partners' pockets while he was asleep or from the corner store. That is until the white man who owned the store finally caught her. However, once Lyric told him her true sob story, he actually allowed her to come in once a month and get free milk, bread and eggs. Sometimes he even allowed her to get a few canned goods. She learned to ration that food to make it last. That's how she was finally able to eat on a regular basis. Lyric was later told by people in the neighborhood, that man was her father. However, that rumor was never confirmed.

People used to pick on her in school and boys never paid her any attention because she always had to wear the same clothes to school for weeks at a time. Even though they didn't have a washing machine, Lyric at least used the hand soap to keep the clothes clean; clothes that she had to borrow from Kendra and were always too big. Even when she started junior high school and met Portia, who Lyric instantly clicked with, she had to borrow from Portia as well.

One day when Lyric got home from school, they had an eviction notice on the door. Her mother hadn't paid the rent in four months, and before Lyric could blink, they were evicted. The sad part about it was, Lyric's mother went out to get a hit one day and never came back, leaving her homeless. Lyric hated her mother for never taking care of her, but she hated her even more now for leaving her, never saying goodbye.

With her survival mode kicking in, Lyric lied about her age and went to a homeless shelter for women for about a week until they got suspicious. Refusing to be placed in the system,

Lyric asked Mama Moses to take her in, and was relieved when she instantly approved.

After living with Portia for awhile, she studied her style and the way Portia was able to snag all the drug dealers. After getting her first drug dealer in high school, Lyric made herself a promise that from that point on, all the men she dated had to have money. She wanted to be rich and live the lifestyle she saw on the movies. She refused to be broke.

Lyric's trip down memory lane was interrupted when she heard the girls cheering as they pulled up in front of the Hilton. She shook it off and got herself together determined not to let her childhood, Diesel or anything else spoil the rest of her night. She grabbed her compact mirror, applied a coat of M.A.C. Viva Glam lip gloss, which was her favorite, fluffed her hair and hopped out. It wasn't long before Portia started doing an excited little dance and the girls started chanting, "Go Portia, go Portia!" Even Kendra and Sheena joined in once they hopped off the bike.

Lyric smiled hoping they were ready to rub the smooth skin that belonged to the six sexy, big dick hung low, male strippers she had waiting for them upstairs. Portia turned around to wait for Lyric after realizing she wasn't with the rest of the crowd.

"I know you not sweating that shit that happened in the club are you?"
Portia asked, putting her arm around Lyric.

Before Lyric could reply, they were distracted by the loud music and cheering sounds coming from The Charlotte Convention Center where a sold out Anthony Hamilton and Musiq Soul Child concert was coming to an end.

"Honestly Portia, I don't care anymore, I'm starting to realize that Diesel doesn't want the same things that I do. So, I've got to figure some shit out and do what's best for me."

"Well, whatever you decide to do, I love you and I'm always here for you. Fuck that cheating bastard. Now, cheer up and let's go watch some dicks bounce!"

"I love you, too," Lyric replied with a smile as they headed inside to get drunk and drop it like it's hot.

The girls arrived upstairs in the luxurious penthouse, which provided a warm and vibrant atmosphere with the most beautiful panoramic view of the city. They all ate cold appetizers that had been sitting there for hours, drank and bonded. However, the more alcohol that flowed, Lyric noticed Kendra's mood start to change.

"You alright, cuz?" Lyric asked when she noticed Kendra drinking heavy and pacing back and forth. She also watched Sheena as she mingled with everyone in the room.

"Yeah, I'm straight," Kendra answered.

Soon after, Lyric went into the bedroom then resurfaced minutes later before generously passing out twenty one-dollar bills to everyone. It didn't matter that she didn't know the women because in Lyric's mind, it wasn't her money to begin with. Besides, she was pissed at Diesel, so giving away his loot made her feel good.

"Get your money ready ladies, as I introduce to you, The Black Steel Male Dancers." Suddenly, the lights went out and you could hear feet slowly stomping to the sounds of, *Tipsy* by Pretty Ricky.

The women screamed when the lights came on and in the middle of the floor stood six of the finest male strippers they'd ever seen. Each one was oiled up with huge erect dicks in multi colored g-strings. Lyric looked for at least one ugly one with some type of flaw, but she couldn't find one. They were all gorgeous. As the strippers began dancing in the middle of the floor, dollar bills began to fall everywhere. They were definitely making it rain.

"Where the fuck did you find these strippers? They all fine as hell. I will definitely be fucking one of them tonight!" Sheena yelled, grabbing one of them by the dick.

"I see why Platinum Management is called the best in the NC. They did their damn thing with these cuties," Lyric agreed. "Damn!" she shouted, noticing one of the strippers lift Portia up in the air and put his face in between her legs.

"I hope you washed!" someone shouted.

Lyric walked around the room making sure all the ladies were enjoying themselves and wasn't at all surprised when she saw Sheena off to the side of the room with one of the strippers in a chair grinding her pussy on his crotch. She then got off him, plopped down on the floor and made her booty clap.

"That bitch always got to be the center of attention. This is not her damn show," Lyric said out loud. As Lyric watched Kendra sitting in the corner looking mad as hell like she was plotting something, Lyric started to wonder if her cousin coming to the party was a good idea.

"Kendra, are you sure everything's cool?" Lyric asked not wanting any drama.

All Lyric got was a head nod yes.

Lyric checked her phone when it vibrated in hopes that Diesel had called to apologize, but it was only one of those stupid marketing emails and she didn't have any missed calls. "I can't believe his bitch-ass hasn't called yet."

Fifteen minutes later, all the drinks had Sheena feeling so fucked up she could hardly walk straight. Needing to go to the bathroom, she quickly made her way past the screaming women still giving up dollars to the strippers and smiled. "Y'all save some for me." Once inside the bathroom, Sheena went to push the door shut, but was stopped by Kendra's boot.

"What the hell are you doing?" Sheena asked. "Can I use the damn bathroom in private please?"

"Oh, so you don't remember me now, huh? You wanna ignore me, huh?" Kendra reached over and grabbed Sheena by the neck and slung her across the bathroom floor, causing her to hit her head on the wall. "What happened to all that shit you were talking to me outside the club? In case you didn't know, I don't play games, bitch!"

Sheena made her way to her feet, feeling dizzy and reluctantly tried to think of a plan. She'd had way too many drinks to fight back. At that moment, Kendra grabbed Sheena by the hair then smacked her across the face causing an immediate burn.

Kendra pushed her elbow into Sheena's chest. "I'm someone you don't wanna ever fuck with." Her eyes bulged out her head like a deranged woman.

Sheena tried to fight back, but was no match for someone who was physically fit. Kendra had even started pumping iron since she came home. The only thing left to do was scream.

"Get off me!" Sheena yelled.

"What the fuck?" Lyric asked when she approached the doorway a few seconds later. "Kendra what are you doing? You're going to kill her!"

Lyric ran and pulled her cousin off Sheena who immediately started talking shit when she knew she had some help. Lyric eventually pushed Sheena out of the bathroom and turned to ask her cousin what was going on.

"I'm sorry, cuz. I guess I gotta lil' carried away, and I might be a little drunk, but that bitch pissed me off. On the way over here, she kept fondling my fucking breasts. Then while we were parking, she kept talking shit about sucking on my clit all night. Then, when we get up here and she sees dicks it's a different story. Don't that bitch know I'm not to be fucked with? She's not gonna get me all horny, then play me. Fuck that."

The thought of Sheena and Kendra doing anything was disgusting to hear, but Lyric knew she had to do it in order to sort things out. "She may be wrong for teasing you, Kendra, but you can't go around beating people because of that. You just got out of prison. Didn't you learn anything?"

Kendra pushed her dreads away from her face. "Yeah, I learned that if a bitch fucks with me in any way, she gotta be dealt with."

"No, you can't do that. Sheena is my friend, Kendra. She's like family. Besides, what you have to understand is that Sheena loves men, too. I don't think you're gonna be able to change that."

It seemed as if Lyric's last choice of words had hit a soft spot. "Yeah, you right. That shit was wrong. I'll go apologize to her." Kendra turned to walk out the bathroom then stopped. "She better be glad, you came to her rescue though because her ass was about to get beat down."

"And your ass would've been going back to prison," Lyric returned.

When the two ladies walked back into the living room, Portia had put everybody out, including the strippers and Sheena.

"Where is everybody?" Lyric asked looking around.

"They're gone," Portia said in a dry tone. "I don't know how Sheena or all those girls are gonna get home, back to the club…wherever and I don't care. Every time we get together, it's some bullshit. I'm getting really tired of all the drama." Portia looked at both Lyric and Kendra. "Thanks, for ruining my bachlorette party. I'm going to bed."

Portia didn't even give Lyric and Kendra a chance to reply before leaving them standing in the living room. They looked like two lost puppies. After Kendra apologized to Lyric for making her friend mad, she grabbed her motorcycle helmet and left as well.

Lyric, Portia and Sheena all had plans to spend the night, but after destroying her friend's special day, Lyric decided to go home. She also wanted to go home to see if Diesel was there. After checking her phone again, and there were no calls, Lyric apologized to Portia, grabbed her over sized purse and headed downstairs to her pearl- white Range Rover. On her way home, she tried to remain calm, but a thousand things kept visualizing in her mind. She couldn't believe Diesel hadn't at least called to give her some sort of excuse. Pulling out her phone, she dialed Diesel's number, but it went straight to voice mail.

"His ass better be at home sleep and just cut his phone off," Lyric tried to convince herself.

She lowered her head for a quick second, feeling defeated. Then suddenly, the old school jam, *OPP* by Naughty by Nature came on the satellite radio

"How ironic," she said. "Diesel is definitely other people's property."

Lyric dialed his number, but was confronted by his voicemail again. Plotting revenge, she punched the accelerator like a mad woman. When she pulled up to her thirty-three hundred square foot home in the upscale neighborhood, Ballantyne, where some of the homes ranged from one to four million, she was shocked once she hit her garage remote. Diesel's car was no where to be found. She felt violated, disrespected and played like a piano.

Knowing there was no reason to call him again, she pulled her truck into the garage, closed the door then walked into the house. After setting the alarm and placing her phone on the charger, she didn't waste anytime slipping out of her clothes and jumping into bed. She was tired, but most of all, hurt. Lyric nestled her body deep under the goose down comforter trying to shut down her thoughts. However, before closing her eyes she mumbled, "I will get you back, Diesel. Trust me on that, and it's gonna be the element of surprise."

# Chapter 4

As soon as Sheena's manicured toes touched her dirty bedroom carpet, she ran at full speed to her bathroom when she felt herself about to vomit. The entire room began to spin as her head thumped like a pulse. She'd obviously drank way too much last night. After turning the knob, Sheena realized the door was locked. Not having time to bang on the door, Sheena ran to Diva's bathroom, making it just in time. She kneeled down on the cold bathroom with her head in the toilet as whatever she'd eaten and drank made it's way back up.

After throwing up what felt like all of her major organs, Sheena grabbed a wash cloth out the small linen closet and wet her face. The cold water felt so good on her skin.

"Damn, I need to slow down on that fucking Tanqueray," she said, looking at the bags under her eyes. She had no idea what time it was, but it was obvious that she hadn't gotten eight hours of beauty rest.

Thinking back to the night before, Sheena remembered when Portia mentioned that Russell was coming back in town for the wedding, she completely lost it. At the time, Sheena remembered feeling her body trembling. She thought she'd gotten past the pain Russell caused her, but it was clear that the possibility of seeing him was too much for her to handle.

Trying to block the potential disaster out of her mind, Sheena made her way back into her room and closed the door, wondering who was in her bathroom. She knew Diva would use it sometimes to take a bath in her Jacuzzi tub, so Sheena decided to go with that conclusion until she suddenly heard a man coughing. Looking in the direction of her bathroom, she wondered what crazy shit she'd done, and with whom? Glancing down at her naked body, Sheena knew it had been a wild night after staring at what appeared to be dried up chocolate all over her chest. She took her finger and tasted it.

"Yeah, it's chocolate," she confirmed.

Sheena was so twisted the night before she couldn't remember anything after arriving at the strip club where she worked, Club Onyx. Knowing she got free drinks, as soon as Sheena walked up to the bar, she started drinking lots of that gin that made people sin. She remembered leaving Portia's party earlier that night already fucked up from the drinks she had there. She ended up having to ditch Kendra who somehow found out where she was and repeatedly followed her around, apologizing. Sheena felt like she might be willing to go out with Kendra, but things had to be on her terms. She could tell that Kendra was jealous and controlling, and wasn't sure if she wanted to deal with that.

Looking around her room, Sheena hated the fact that she'd just done who knows what and didn't even know the guy's name. Soon, her attention was drawn to his trail of clothes. She picked up a pair of expensive Ferragamo shoes, and frowned. They were small; a size eight to be exact.

"Damn, that's small. Normally the dudes I fuck with wear at least a twelve. I wonder if he had a little dick," she said to herself. A few steps over she saw his True Religion jeans, noticing they were also small; a thirty-three waist. "Shit, I hope I didn't fuck a Gary Coleman type of nigga."

However, from the looks of his clothes he was probably stacking paper. She knew those shoes were at least four hundred and some change. "I at least hope he's fine because liquor will make an ugly man look hella good," Sheena said.

She reached in his pockets and felt a large knot, which instantly made her smile. She was a blood hound when it came to money, and the scent of currency in the air always made her feel good. She peeled off a few bills from the middle, that way it wasn't as easy to detect. Sleeping with men and stealing their money was something she was known for. She quickly placed the stolen bills in her purse and the knot back in his pants as soon as she heard the guy moving around. When the door opened a few seconds later, Sheena almost lost her mind when she saw who it was.

*Oh, shit, what the hell did I do*, she thought after covering her mouth. She watched as Diesel made his way over toward her. His dick, which wasn't that big like she thought, swung from side to side. He even had the nerve to smile before sitting down on the bed.

"What up, Ma? You sleep good?"

At that moment, Sheena rushed over to her closet and grabbed her oversized Washington Redskins sweat shirt, then threw it on. "Oh, my God. Diesel, you have to get the hell out of here. What if Lyric stops by?" She grabbed his clothes and threw them to him.

"Girl, what the hell you trippin' for now? You weren't concerned about Lyric last night when we had sex for hours."

"I obviously had too much to drink last night. If it weren't for that you wouldn't be here right now!" Sheena placed her hand on her pounding head. Now, she really had a headache. Please leave, Diesel," she pleaded.

"Relax, I'll leave after you get over here and ride this dick. If you don't, I'll tell Lyric you came on to me at the strip club. You know she'll forgive me, but you on the other hand will have a serious problem if she finds out." Sheena couldn't believe that he was blackmailing her. "Now, get that fat-ass over here and I'll be on my way. Then we can forget this shit ever happened."

# LOVE HEIST

Sheena never gave a damn about sleeping with someone else's husband or boyfriend, but Lyric was her friend and she never crossed the line with her friends. She felt bad…really bad.

"Come on bitch, my dick is hard as a rock," Diesel said, laying back on the bed. "Real talk. You should've thought about Lyric before you were all up in my face arguin' about my other girl at Club Onyx last night. You piped down as soon as I started givin' yo' ass some Patron though."

Sheena wiped away a single tear as she took the sweat shirt back off and climbed in bed on top of Diesel. She closed her eyes tight trying not to look at him or deal with the heartless thing she'd done to her friend. This was an all time low for her.

After placing Diesel's little dick inside of her, Sheena moved up and down a bit, but it wasn't like her normal stallion routine. She could ride a dick good, but wasn't trying to show Diesel her skills.

"Throw that pussy back at me like you did last night, bitch. The quicker you make me cum, the quicker I'm up out of here," Diesel demanded.

Sheena started moving her hips and twisting her ass. At that moment, she had a flashback of her father making her do a similar act to him when she a teenager. That's when the tears really began to flow.

Suddenly, Diesel grabbed her ass and pushed his dick inside of her. "Stop playin' around. I know you fuck better than that!"

Trying to make him cum so it would be over, Sheena decided to grind her pussy nice and hard. After doing a few of her famous moves, Diesel finally began to jerk, which meant he was finally finished. Instantly, Sheena hopped off him and tossed him his clothes for the second time.

"You got what you want, now leave."

He reached in his pocket and pulled out the same wad of money and peeled off some more cash and handed the bills to Sheena. "You did your thing last night, real talk. I want to do this shit again, Lyric doesn't have to know." He reached on the night stand and grabbed Sheena's iPhone and locked his number in.

Suddenly, the bedroom door opened and her daughter, Diva walked in. "Sheena, I need you to take me to..."

Sheena, who still laid butt naked, jumped up. "Why did you just barge in my room? Get out!"

Diva looked at Diesel who was now zipping up his jeans. "You slept with Diesel? Oh, my God. I'm telling Auntie Lyric!"

Diesel walked over to Diva and grabbed her ponytail. "If you or yo' mother opens yo' mouth, trust me you'll regret it. Plus I'm the one who gives Lyric the money to buy yo' ass all that shit, so you wouldn't want to fuck up that. Do you understand me?"

"Yes," Diva said, pulling her hair from his grip.

"Okay then keep yo' fuckin' mouth shut. Yo' mother and I ran into each other last night at her job and we both had way too much to drink. We didn't mean for this to happen." He then peeled off four hundred dollars and gave it Diva. She was hesitant to take it before Diesel gave her a stern look. "We all straight here?" he asked.

"Yes," they both said in a weak tone.

After putting on the rest of his clothes, Diesel reached over and smacked Sheena on the ass. "Don't forget about my offer," he said and left the room.

There was an uncomfortable silence for what seemed like forever before Diva finally spoke up. "I hope you not planning to see Diesel again. You not right Sheena, you need to stop drinking," Diva shook her head in disgust.

"Who the fuck you calling, Sheena? I'm tired of you doing that. It's Ma to you. You're not grown yet Diva, you're only sixteen. Besides, you need to worry about them men your hot-ass is having sex with; not my business. Get out my room anyway. You got it twisted around here, I'm the mother, you're the daughter!" Sheena yelled.

Diva walked out her mother's room and slammed the door.

# LOVE HEIST

Sheena lowered her head as tears began to fall once again. She was devastated and didn't know what to do. Already knowing what Lyric had to go through, Sheena's heart ached. The more she thought about what had just happened, the worst she felt.

Feeling like there was nowhere else to turn, Sheena jumped up then made her way to the bathroom to take a shower. Twenty minutes later, she was dressed in her multi print Marc Jacobs dress that fit every curve of her body along with her platform Pedro Garcia pumps and left for Club Onyx. The only thing that was going to make her feel better at the moment was a drink.

# Chapter 5

The next morning, Russell was awakened when he heard the loud voice of a staff member over the intercom. "All inmates report to the recreation area for breakfast."

He didn't bother getting up because he never liked the prison food. He liked to cook his own meals with the use of the microwave located in his old dorm. Russell was so good, many of inmates called him, Chef King. Known for his tasty nachos, burritos, and tuna pasta, his favorite meal of all time was fried rice. Inmates along with the C.O.'s sometimes were amazed at how he would take a bag of rice, sausage, seasoning from the oodles of noodles package, a can of Coca Cola and hook up a meal that tasted like it came straight from P.F. Changs.

"Man, I need to get back to my old cell block," Russell said as he laid in bed thinking about his cooking skills.

A few minutes later, he heard, "Russell King, its time for breakfast. We have, eggs, bacon, and fried potatoes, so get up. We all eat at the same time in my unit." He raised his head and saw Liyah standing in his door way with her hands on her wide hips.

*Damn, she looks even better today,* Russell said to himself noticing she'd gotten her hair done. The long sandy colored weave with golden high lights complemented her complexion.

"Let's go, I don't have all day," she said impatiently.

"I've been thinking, if you the nurse, why do you do the job of the C.O.'s? Shouldn't they be the one's harassing inmates?" Russell smiled.

*I'm really in here just to see you*, Liyah thought. "I do my rounds at breakfast, so I just make their job easier by making sure the inmates are up."

"Oh, well I'm not going to eat that nasty-ass food."

"Why not? You should be starving."

"Because I'm so tired of powered eggs and potatoes I don't know what the fuck to do. The potatoes are either fried or in a hashbrown form. Oh, and they might give us a stinking-ass boiled egg every now and then." Russell shook his head. "I mean why can't they get creative. What about a potato casserole with bacon, cheese and onions or a spinach and potato frittata with garlic and a bit of milk?" Just thinking about the food he had in his pile of memorized recipes had his mouth watering.

"Wow, you seem to really know about food."

Russell smiled again. "Yeah, I do. You need to let me cook you some of my famous mackerel cakes. See, I take a can of mackerel and dice it up, add some onions and green peppers, which is contraband by the way. Then I add mayonnaise, and some crackers to hold the cake together, mix it all in a bowl, cook them in the microwave for three minutes on each side, and bam…it's done." He got excited whenever he talked about food.

For once, Liyah enjoyed an inmate's conversion. "I find you really interesting. It's nothing worse than being around crazy-ass men with crazy-ass conversations."

Russell cut his eye in her direction, "Nothing crazy over here baby, just somebody misunderstood," he said, getting out the bed revealing his naked body. His big dick swung from side to side.

Liyah quickly turned around. "Umm. Mr. King, you're not supposed to sleep in the nude. That's against our policy."

"Why not? I'm in the cell by myself." Russell smiled.

"Besides, you like what you see?"

Liyah wanted so badly to say yes, but didn't want to lose her job. "I'm gonna step out Mr. King. Put your clothes on now!" Liyah walked out slowly trying to act as if she didn't steal one final look.

Russell turned around and bent over. Grabbing his jumpsuit and shoes, he put everything on before heading to the bathroom to brush his teeth. Liyah's eyes skimmed over his back, broad shoulders and tight ass. She wanted to go rub her hands through his thick curly hair. With his bushy eyebrows, and cinnamon complexion, Russell was a dead ringer for the actor, Allen Payne, better known as G Money from the movie, *New Jack City*.

"He's tall, dark, handsome and thuggish just the way I like my men. Ummmm," she said to herself. However, even though the inmates got on her nerves, it wouldn't be the first time she'd been attracted to one. She stood for a minute reminiscing about Russell masturbating the night before when she was just about to go home. She wasn't even supposed to be anywhere near the cells, but had to get one final peek at him before she left. It was something about him that turned her on. *He don't look crazy like the rest of these muthafuckas and I'm horny. I really must be desperate, lusting over a damn inmate.* Suddenly, Liyah felt a tingling in her panties, and closed her eyes, took a deep breath and counted to ten to get herself together. She snapped out of it and joined the rest of the inmates in the dining hall.

Ten minutes later, Russell took his fork and stabbed at the stiff eggs. He did manage to eat the bacon and two pieces of bread, but wasn't looking forward to lunch. On a good day, they normally had greasy-ass fried chicken. On a bad day, it was meatloaf with some secret unknown ingredients. Drinking his last bit of orange juice, Russell looked over and noticed the big dude he noticed the day before, watching him. It made him feel edgy. When the guy continued to stare, Russell jumped up with his folk in his hand.

"What the fuck you looking at?" Russell asked. The big dude never said a word. Russell eyed the big guy's thick afro that looked as if it hadn't been picked out in years, and his massive stomach through the too small jumpsuit. "Yo, dog, this aint what you want nigga!" he continued. Russell began sweating and breathing deeply, but then thought of his release date coming up. Telling himself to calm down, he quickly shook his head. "They trying me up in this muthafucka."

Suddenly, the big dude mumbled something under his breath.

When Russell thought he heard him say, "Fuck you, faggot," he instantly went off. "Nigga, what did you just say to me?"

The dude stood up and looked down on Russell. "I said fuck you faggot. I run this unit so you better sit your ass down before I tear your damn face off!"

Russell looked around the dinning hall for something to hit the massive guy with. The first thing he saw was a food tray. Not even hesitating, he picked it up and ran up to the guy, smashing the tray in his face.

As soon as the guy realized what happened, he ran toward Russell, but was met by a vicious right hook. He stumbled backwards. Russell walked up on him and hit him with another right hook, then a left. At that point, the dude grabbed Russell by his shirt and body slammed him on the floor several times like a professional wrestler. It was obvious the guy was tired by the way he began to sweat profusely. In return, Russell grabbed him by the neck and punched him in the throat. The two fought for almost ten minutes until Liyah finally came running in.

"What are you two retards in here fighting about?" She looked at Russell. "How stupid can you be, fucking up your chances to get out of here?"

As soon as Liyah made that statement, Russell immediately stopped. He hopped up off the big guy and walked a few feet away. Liyah quickly looked at the ward. "You both got about a minute to clean this shit up before the C.O's come. I suggest you hurry up and work together or you both will have some time added to your sentences." She eyed Russell again. "I'm trying to look out for you. Don't make me regret my decision. Clean this mess up while I try and distract the C.O's."

Russell looked at the dude who was already cleaning up and putting the tables in place. He joined in and picked up some of the spilled food. *I'm not trying to stay in this ward with that crazy muthafucka any longer than I have to, so I'm willing to do whatever. Besides, the next time, shit is not gonna go that smoothly.*

❤❤❤❤❤❤❤

Later that afternoon, Russell sat impatiently in the recreation room glancing up at the big iron clock on the wall every few seconds, realizing he was late for his appointment with Dr. O'Malley. Suddenly, the big dude who Russell had just gotten into it with during breakfast came over and sat in the chair beside him. "Here comes this mutherfucka," Russell said, as he sat up looking around for a weapon. He was ready to fight. "Fuck getting out if this nigga try some shit again."

The dude started off with his normal staring, but then finally said something. "I'm Big Country, what you in foe?" he asked, with a deep country accent.

Russell looked at him. *Didn't we just go to blows this morning? Why is he even talking to me?* He stared at the guy for a second. "Second degree murder. Why?" He looked at Big Country's untamed mustache.

"Cuz I'm in here for attempted murder. I ran over one of my trainers with my SUV cuz he threatened to report my steroid use. I almost killed 'em. I wish I had doe, cuz the nosy mutherfucker was always in my business. Then, I beat a fan to death for tapin' me on 'da shoulder askin' for a fuckin' autograph."

Russell began to lighten up a bit. He thought his case was bad. "Damn."

"Yeah, man I was using steroids hard, and they had me

trippin'. I tried to tell 'da judge 'dat 'dem steroids had me delusional, but I guess he won't tryna hear 'dat shit."

"So, you said something about your fans. What do you do? Or should I say what *did* you do?"

"I'ma defensive full back foe the Miami Dolphins. All I got to do is get clean, and do these years, and hopefully I'll be back in football trainin' camp next season," Big Country stated.

"Hold up. Curtis Burston, right? I knew you looked familiar," Russell announced, pointing his finger. "I seen a couple of games where you were ripping niggas heads off on the field."

"Yeah, 'dats me. I miss playin' ball, man. That's all a country boy like me love."

Russell thought for a second. "Hold up, that was like five years ago when you were playing."

"I know. I got caught out there, but when I start playin' again, I'ma be on the straight and fuckin' narrow."

Russell wanted to say, *dude, ain't no way in hell they're gonna let your crazy-ass back on somebody's field after five years*, but decided not to go there. "You might be able to play again. As good as you were, I'm sure another team will pick you up," Russell lied.

"Oh, hell yeah. Somebody gonna pick me up foe sure. I'ma be out there smashin' dem dudes." Big Country began hitting his massive arms.

Russell shook his head. *This muthafucka really is delusional.*

Seconds later, Big Country noticed Russell watching the clock impatiently. "Those guards be takin' their time comin' to get us foe appointments. That shit be havin' me heated. They ain't forget 'bout you, dog."

"Russell King. Let's go Russell we're late," Russell heard two male C.O.'s call out letting him know they were finally there to escort him.

"See, these muthafucka's late, and now they wanna rush you," Big Country said.

"Stay out of this, Curtis. We don't want any shit out of

you," one C.O. replied.

When Big Country stood up displaying his huge 6'6'
height, the C.O.'s looked like they were getting themselves
ready for battle. It was obvious that Big Country was known for
starting shit.

"Punk-ass muthafuckas. Just like my trainer," Big Country announced. He looked at Russell before walking back to his
cell. "Later, dog."

Russell stood up as the C.O.'s placed him in handcuffs.
Once he was secure, they unlocked the door to Unit A then proceeded down the hallway escorting Russell through Unit B.
Liyah was right; the rest of the psych ward was unbearable. The
strong foul smell of piss assaulted Russell's nose immediately.
He wondered how anybody could stay or work in those condi-
tions. While waiting for the elevator, Russell looked over and
watched as an inmate stood at the window of his cell eating his
own feces. A few seconds later, he smeared it all over the glass
like it was paint.

*Damn, I got to get the fuck up outta here,* Russell thought
stepping on the elevator.

When they finally made it to the third floor, the C.O's led
Russell to Dr. O'Malley's small dusty office, then stood outside
the door like guards from the series Prison Break. Seconds later,
Russell could see C.O. Douglas looking inside the room at him
and talking to the other C.O.'s at the same time. He had a black
eye, a bandage across his right cheek, and a neck brace.

*Hold up. Nurse Liyah didn't say shit about a neck brace.
She said I broke his arm. Plus, I thought they fired his ass.* Russell thought. Based on the C.O's injuries, things weren't looking
so good. He started feeling nervous. "Now, I'm probably never
getting out." However, he was especially nervous when C. O.
Douglas looked back into the room and Russell read his lips.

"You will never get out of here if I can help it."

# Chapter 6

A smile that could only represent true happiness spread across Russell's face when he heard the door open, and saw Dr. O'Malley making her way inside. She was a gorgeous, tall, half-Italian and half black woman with tan skin and long thick hair; hair that she'd recently dyed blonde. Walking in wearing a conservative business suit, and carrying a file folder, Dr. O'Malley sat down at her desk and peered over her wire framed glasses, that made her look educated. Every time Russell had a session with her, he always found himself staring at her large breasts, that couldn't be ignored. With a true talent at spotting a fake pair of silicone tits anywhere, he could tell right away that hers were real.

"Hello, Russell King. How are you feeling?" Dr. O'Malley opened her file and started reading.

"I was good until I woke up in the psych ward, doc. What's up with that?" Russell asked, scratching his face. By not being able to get to the prison barber shop over the past few days, his beard had started to come in.

"Mr. King, before we get to the recent altercation you were involved in, I have to ask you some other questions. Now, you'll quickly realize that these will be questions that you and I

51

have already discussed in our past sessions, but the parole board has advised me to ask them one last time. Do you understand?"

Russell wanted to say "no" so badly, but as soon as she mentioned the parole board, all that changed. He even sat up a little straighter in the chair. "Yes."

"Does mental illness run in your family?" Dr. O'Malley asked while jotting down some notes.

Russell thought about her question and contemplated about whether he was supposed to lie or be honest. He also couldn't remember what he'd told the doctor before. Russell remembered his mother also being diagnosed with schizophrenia when he was very young. She used to have hallucinations and would call for him to come sit with her and talk until her antipsychotic meds took effect and the voices had stopped. His mom stayed in and out of the hospital until one day she refused to go back; even stopped taking her medication. From there, that's when her drug abuse started.

"Russell, did you hear my question?"

"No, mental illness doesn't run in my family," Russell responded, knowing it was a lie. He never liked to talk about his mother or her situation to anyone. The only people who knew were his cousin Portia and his grandmother, Mama Moses who ended up raising both of them.

"Russell, tell me how you feel since your wife's death."

"I was hurt. She was planning to leave me. Seems like every woman I love, leaves me. That's why I had so many women. Bitches ain't shit but hoe's and tricks." Russell recited from a popular rap song by Snoop Dogg.

"Go on," Dr. O'Malley said, as she continued writing notes.

"I shoulda drugged her ass up and fucked the shit outta her and kept it moving when we first met." He began to tap his foot rapidly.

Dr. O' Malley stopped writing and looked over her reading glasses, once again.

"If you're telling me you have drugged women and had

sex with them, that's rape, I'll have to report this."

Russell had to think fast. He cursed at himself for allow-ing that last part to slip out.

"Oh, no I'm not talking about nothing major. I'm talking about that Ecstasy pill. That's what everybody was doing before I got locked up. See, I have a sexual drive that most women can't handle. I have to release at least three straight orgasms be-fore my dick will even go down. Sometimes they last for hours. Trust me, the drugging thing was consensual."

Russell knew his lie would have her squirming in her seat. Dr. O'Malley wrote a few more notes in the file and closed it thinking to herself, *Damn, I need a man like that at home. I'm sick of my husband with his two minute-ass.* She quickly shook it off.

"You shouldn't talk like that, Mr. King. People may take the whole drugging thing out of context." Russell nodded his head in agreement. "Now, is there anything else you wish to share with me before C.O. Douglas comes in? We need to talk about the incident. Normally, you would've had this discussion with Warden Grimes, but he asked me to do it since you and I have had previous sessions. He felt as though you might open up to me a little more."

Russell wanted to tell her about his recent anxiety and audible hallucinations about his wife, but he was afraid that in-formation would only hurt his situation. He decided it was best to keep it to himself. "No, nothing else."

Moments later, C.O. Douglas walked in. This time, Rus-sell noticed that he was in plain clothes and wearing a cast on his arm. He tried to display a look of innocence, but Russell knew better than to fall for that. As C.O. Douglas sat in the chair beside him, Russell still wondered what was up with the neck brace. *He probably doesn't want anyone to know that he's a red-neck*, Russell joked to himself.

"C.O. Douglas would you like to start?" Dr. O'Malley asked.

"First of all, just call me Douglas," the guard replied.

"Secondly, I don't have much to say other than this animal shouldn't be getting out anytime soon. I mean look at what he did to me?" Douglas held up the fresh white cast.

Dr. O'Malley looked over her glasses. "Douglas, let's reframe from any name calling during this meeting. You're only here to give your side of the story." She looked at Russell. "Mr. King would you like to say something?"

Russell cleared his throat. He had to choose his words wisely. "Well, I just want to say that C.O. Douglas doesn't need to work here anymore because he's a raci…" Russell paused for a moment. "He's not fair to the black inmates. He started the altercation by throwing something at me, which was completely disrespectful."

Douglas stood up and began to turn beet red. "You're fucking lying. Just like all these other inmates who have complaints against me. I didn't throw shit at you. You hit me first, nigga!"

When Dr. O'Malley's eyes widened, Douglas knew he'd fucked up. "Sorry for the name calling again, but you just don't understand. This man threatened to kill me! I mean, look what ward he's in now. Doesn't that mean anything?"

"Douglas, I think we're done here," the doctor replied.

"So, what's going to happen?" Douglas inquired.

She looked at Russell's file again. "Well, Warden Grimes has plans to review the tape of the incident in his office today. After that, I'll give him my recommendation, and he'll relay our decision to the Parole Board."

This time Douglas' eyes widened. "Tape?"

"Yes, of course. It's not like the facility isn't being monitored at all times, Douglas, did you forget about that?" Dr. O'Malley inquired.

Russell smiled then thought, *Douglas was so pissed off, he probably did.*

The doctor looked at Douglas, who quickly turned his head. "Is that all, Douglas?" she asked.

"Yeah." Douglas didn't hesitate turning around, knocking on the door to let his fellow officers know that the meeting was over, then walked out.

At that moment, both the doctor and Russell proceeded toward the door as well. As Russell slightly brushed up against her, she looked down at his crouch when she felt the large bulge in the front of his pants. Russell looked at her nipples sticking out of her blouse due to the drafty room. He licked his lips after getting a closer look at her breasts. He wanted to suck them…badly.

When Dr. O'Malley noticed Russell looking at her chest, she closed her suit jacket trying to keep things professional. "Goodbye, Mr. King. I'll be in touch." She turned around and walked down the opposite end of the hallway.

Two hours after lights out, Russell was awakened by the sound of keys and footsteps moving around in his room. He jumped up wondering if it was another psychotic episode. He'd been having bad dreams about his wife, so for all he knew, she was now coming into his room. Russell was just about to see what she wanted when he suddenly heard a female's voice say, "Here, put one of these condoms on." Rubbing his eyes to make sure he wasn't dreaming, he realized it was Liyah as she tossed him several Magnums.

"You don't have to beat your meat tonight," she said, rushing up on him. It wasn't long before she reached inside his pants pulling out his dick.

Russell was fully awake now; he loved a woman that took charge, but also didn't want to get caught. "Hold up, you can't be in here."

"You think I don't know that. Don't worry, I know the C.O. on duty, and he ain't trippin', especially since I just hooked him up with my sister. Now, let's go. We don't have all night."

Liyah's confirmation was good enough for him. At that point, Russell quickly slid the magnum condom over his thick meat ready to blow her back out. He then pulled her white pants down, and instantly became aroused once he realized that she wasn't wearing any panties. In the dark cell, Russell couldn't see like he wanted, but could feel every nook and cranny. Her pubic hairs were definitely groomed.

Quickly bending Liyah over the bed, Russell entered her from behind in a slow pace. She moaned once his ten-inch dick began thrusting hard and fast. He took control, driving in and out and hitting all the right spots. He reached around and pulled on her breast while talking dirty in her ear. The harder she moaned, the faster his strokes got. Liyah's heavy breathing turned Russell on. Moments later, Liyah covered her mouth as she approached a powerful orgasm. Listening to her reaching her climax, it wasn't long before Russell shot a load of cum into the condom. Both of their bodies began to shake uncontrollably. Liyah felt whipped instantly.

After pulling her pants back up, she gave him two quick pecks on his cheek, then made her way toward the door. "Be ready, I'll be back tomorrow night."

This routine continued the next three nights, causing both Liyah and Russell to be on cloud nine. She'd even been sneaking some of Russell's favorite foods inside his cell. She also managed to get Russell's mail from his old cell block, which he was excited about; even more so, when he opened a letter from Portia.

*What up, Cuz?*

*I hope this letter find's you in good health. You said in your last letter that you should be getting out around the time of my wedding. I hope that's still the case. If so, remember the date is April 24th. Let me know if you need some help getting back to Charlotte. I sent you an invitation to the prison, but it was returned for some reason. I know you can't wait to get out of that place…lol. I hope you get this message in time to make my wedding. It won't be the same without you. Can't wait for you to meet Charles. I Love You.*

*Portia*

"Damn, I hope I will be able to make it. I wouldn't want to miss Portia's wedding for anything. I just pray the nigga she with know he got an angel and I'll kill his ass if he mistreats her," Russell said to himself.

After putting the letter back, he began looking at the April issue of his Don Diva magazine subscription, when he saw Dr. O'Malley walking into his cell. Holding a legal sized brown envelope in her hand, she made her way over toward Russell with a blank expression. He hoped like hell she had good news.

"Well, Mr. King, congratulations. Due to the evidence on the tape during the incident with you and C.O. Douglas, along with the information I gave Warden Grimes about the racist slur he called you, and my recommendation, the parole board decided not to overturn their decision. It looks like you'll be a free man, in exactly one week. April 21st is still the official date."

Russell jumped up and scooped Dr. O'Malley off her feet. "Yes, oh my God. Thank you. Thank you!"

"Please put me down, Mr. King," the doctor replied. She was happy for him, but didn't want anyone to walk by and get the wrong impression.

Russell's smile was wider than a football field. "I can't believe this."

"It's true. C.O. Douglas was discharged, so I guess that's good news as well." She placed the envelope in his hand. "Well, I guess this is it. I wish you nothing but success. As long as you don't end up back in here, you'll be fine." She patted Russell on his shoulder, then made her way toward the door. "My office is always open just in case you need to see me before you go."

Opening up the envelope, Russell's jaw dropped once he saw what was inside. It was a note from Dr. O'Malley along with a pair of red lace thongs.

*Look me up when you get on the outside. I've been wanting to fuck the shit out of you for years.*

"Shit," Russell said, picking up her thong. He held it to his nose. "If her pussy tastes as good as it smells, that shit must be good," he said, after another hard sniff. He placed the panties back in the envelope. "I'm definitely keeping these as a souvenir."

Along with the panties and the note, there was also a prescription for Zyprexa, a drug for bipolar disorder. He had plans to keep the prescription too, even though he wasn't planning on taking the meds. In his mind, he could handle anything and no doctor or pill was going to tell him otherwise.

A week later, Russell finally walked out of Coleman Federal Correctional Facility a free man. Liyah had a cab waiting for him outside the gate to take him straight to her house. While riding, he looked around at all the people out and about enjoying their freedom. He rolled down the window so he could feel the sunshine on his face. After being locked up for sixteen years, he learned not to take small things like that for granted. He admired all the new cars out on the road, telling himself that as soon as he got on his feet, he would have a new whip along with a new wardrobe of course.

The cab pulled into a nice subdivision forty minutes later in a town called Spring Hill and pulled up in the driveway of a nice stucco exterior one level home. The garage came up seconds later and Liyah walked out wearing a cute black sundress and smiling from ear to ear. While she paid the cab driver, Russell looked around and saw an ML 320 Benz truck parked in the garage. *Hmmm...not bad. Not bad at all. Guess I was wrong about her living in the hood.*

Liyah noticed that Russell was still sitting in the car. "What are you waiting for? Get out. You're out of prison now. You don't have to wait on anybody to tell you what to do."

Russell got out and followed her into the house expecting all her kids to come running over on some "Are you our new daddy bullshit." But to his surprise he was wrong about that as well. As it turned out, not only did Liyah not have any kids, but she also had a beautiful three bedroom home with stainless steel appliances, nice hardwood floors, and several flat screen T.V's, which amazed Russell. Up until now, he'd only seen them in magazines and on commercials.

Liyah even had dinner already cooked. She'd paid attention to all the foods Russell told her he missed while in prison, and had them all waiting. Baked salmon, mac and cheese, collard greens and iced tea. She'd even baked him a red velvet cake.

He watched Liyah as she fixed his plate. She was fine as hell, nice body and doing well for herself. But he wondered why she was single.

He rubbed his dick as he continued watching her ass shake in that dress, driving him crazy.

"I'm going to tear that ass up," Russell said to himself.

An hour later, they ate, and drank a bottle of white wine before Liyah told Russell to go up stairs and make himself comfortable. "I'll be right up."

Following her directions, Russell headed upstairs and immediately took all his clothes off and collapsed on Liyah's king-size platform bed. After years of sleeping uncomfortably, it felt as if he was laying in mid air. Russell grabbed the remote and turned the television on. The bed felt so good it wasn't long before he fell asleep.

When Liyah finally entered the room and saw Russell sound asleep, she quietly removed her dress and climbed on top of him sliding his big dick inside her moist pussy. Immediately taking charge, she slowly rode his dick grinding her pussy on him with every stroke. Russell opened his eyes.

"That feels good, baby," he moaned.

After moving her hips in a circular motion, Liyah felt herself about to cum. She jumped off not wanting to have an orgasm so fast. She then slid down and put Russell's dick in her mouth sucking it with aggression. She sucked and licked his balls like they were popsicles.

"Damn, Liyah you know how to make a nigga go crazy."

Removing his manhood from her mouth, Liyah slid back up and placed her breasts in Russell's mouth. The way he licked her nipples made her shiver.

"Suck 'em harder, Daddy!" Liyah yelled.

At that moment, Russell had an instant flashback, when Liyah called him by that name; a name that his wife used to call him all the time. He felt the sweat building up on his forehead. Then the voices appeared. *That's why I'm in love with someone else. You can't hurt me. Go ahead...try it. See if you can hurt me.* Obeying what he'd just heard, Russell bit down on Liyah's breast trying to bite her nipple off.

"Ouchhhh! What the fuck is wrong with you?" She screamed, trying to push Russell off her. He still had a tight grip on her breast in his mouth.

Liyah looked at the crazy blank expression on his face and knew she had to talk him out of whatever had triggered his change of behavior. She'd been in this same situation several times at work, so she knew exactly what to do. "Russell, this is me Liyah. What's wrong?" She bit down on her bottom lip try-ing to take her mind of the pain from the grip Russell still had on her now bleeding right breast. "Russell?"

After a few minutes passed, Russell released his grip and got up off the bed retrieving his clothes. He quickly put them back on.

"Where are you going?" Liyah asked holding her bleed-ing breast. She looked down, analyzing the deep teeth marks. *What the hell have I gotten myself into?*

In Russell's mind, Liyah was now the enemy. "Bitch, don't ask me no questions, give me some money, so I can get the fuck up outta here; before I kill you!"

Liyah couldn't believe his tone. She also couldn't believe how he'd just flipped out, but she shouldn't have been surprised. "What? I'm not giving you anything. The only thing you're going get from me, is a one way ticket back to the psycho ward with a violation of parole charge."

At that moment, Russell looked on the nightstand and

spotted her purse. Just like the thief he used to be, he grabbed it, taking out her wallet, which surprisingly had about two hundred dollars inside and her cell phone. He would've tried to take her Benz, but knew a stolen car wouldn't get him very far. However, he did take her keys just in case she tried to follow him.

Liyah jumped up and tried to grab her wallet, but Russell pushed her down on the floor. "No, please, don't do this. Whatever I did, I'm sorry."

"You're just like all the rest!"

Liyah wondered who Russell was talking about. "Just like who? Why don't I go to the drug store and fill your prescription? You're probably just tired and need some rest."

"I don't need anything, bitch. Not you, not my mother, not anybody!" Russell moved toward Liyah like he was about to hit her.

Liyah threw up her hands to protect herself. "No, please."

Russell ignored her cries. "If you call them people on me or have anything to do with fucking with my parole, trust me, I'll kill you bitch," Russell said, on his way out the door.

An hour later, he sat in the back of a Greyhound Bus ready for the eighteen hour drive to Charlotte. He pulled out his notebook and started writing down a few things that kept jumping around in his mind.

*I can't wait to see Portia and I hope Lyric is ready to be my new wife.*

Russell had been in love with Lyric ever since he first laid eyes on her...she just didn't know it. However, after all this time he had plans to be with her regardless of what it took. Nothing or nobody was going to stand in his way.

# Chapter 7

Lyric blinked her eyes to fight back the tears as she heard the pastor say "I now pronounce you man and wife. You may kiss the bride." She wiped the mascara from the corners of her eyes and watched Portia walking out the church with her new husband as Mr. and Mrs. Charles Edwards. Portia looked absolutely beautiful in her strapless A-line gown with tons of swarovski crystals along the bodice. *Mama Moses would really be proud of her granddaughter if she was still alive,* Lyric thought.

As she walked out on the arm of Charles' best friend, dreams about her own wedding day began to consume her mind. Lyric always had visions of herself and all the bridesmaids wearing beautiful dresses designed by Vera Wang and the men in custom made Armani tuxedos. She also had visions of the ceremony and reception filled with red and white roses, and taking place in the Grand Ballroom of the Omni Hotel; a facility known for its exquisite European décor, sixteen-foot ceilings with crystal chandeliers, and dramatic floor-to-ceiling windows, which offered romantic views of uptown Charlotte. She could even picture Diesel standing there looking at her as she walked down the isle, looking like the perfect wife.

Suddenly, Lyric heard Portia's aunt yelling at her bad-ass kids, which quickly brought her back to reality. *Wishful thinking*, Lyric thought to herself with visions of the episode with Diesel at the club still fresh in her mind.

Diesel and Lyric had been engaged off and on for the past two years, and she knew he wasn't ready for marriage. The fact that she constantly caught him cheating let her know they weren't on the same page. Lately, all they did was bump heads. She knew he loved her, and only gave her a ring to lock her down and keep her content for awhile, but that was no longer going to work. She looked down at her five-carat, solitaire Platinum ring with three rows of natural pink diamonds on the band, questioning herself why she continued to stay. The only reason why she even had it on at the moment was because it matched her pink bridesmaid's dress perfectly. She definitely wasn't trying to put on a front.

Over the past two weeks, Diesel had been completely ignoring her feelings about the woman she'd seen him with at the club. After coming home at eight o'clock the next morning, he gave Lyric some lame excuse about being drunk and falling asleep over one of his boy's house, but still didn't give a reason as to why his phone was off. Since then, he continued to come home late almost every night and didn't even bother to show up at the wedding. His only way of apologizing was to bring home a brand new silver Mercedes Benz SLK 55 AMG with dual pipes. When he was in the dog house, the only way Diesel knew how to get out was to buy Lyric whatever she wanted. Little did he know, the one thing she wanted didn't cost a thing…love.

Lyric was tired of the bullshit, the lies, and the lifestyle. She was glad Portia didn't have to deal with drama with her new husband; the infamous Charles Edwards, who was a successful investment banker. She watched as Charles and Portia greeted their guests in the church's lobby with huge smiles. Charles was a good man, and Portia deserved to be happy. Lyric only wished that one day she could find that same joy.

After taking the wedding photos, Lyric stood in the large arched doorway and watched as the newlyweds pulled away from the church headed to Charlotte-Douglas International airport for Maui, Hawaii. Lyric was relieved they'd decided not to have a wedding reception. She wasn't in the mood to sit at a large wedding party table socializing with the family. Hell, it was even weird how Portia wanted the wedding to be on a Sunday. It wasn't like Charles didn't have enough money for a Saturday celebration. During the wedding ceremony she even noticed Sheena hung over from an obvious wild party from the night before, trying her best to hold it together. Lyric was tired of her selfish ass, too. Just like Diesel, Sheena was always fucking up and making excuses afterwards, something that Lyric no longer wanted to condone.

Waiting for the right opportunity, Lyric grabbed her belongings and slipped out the side door unnoticed. She then turned her head as she walked past some of the family and guests standing outside. Once she was alone inside her car, Lyric fought to keep the tears back. She flipped the mirror on the sun visor down and looked at herself whispering, "Why me?" She hit the steering wheel over and over now shouting, "This should be my wedding day, why can't I have the glamorous lifestyle with a man that will be true to me?"

After hitting the steering wheel several more times, Lyric quickly pulled herself together; she was too strong to let anybody see her crumble like that. She rubbed her hands across her face and wiped her tears away. She reached for her Gucci sunglasses and placed them on her face to cover her bloodshot eyes. Lyric was just about to pull out of the parking lot, when she spotted a familiar face walking toward her car. She'd noticed the same man sitting in the back of the church staring her down during the wedding ceremony, but still couldn't figure out who it was. Suddenly, the man walked up to the car and knocked on her window.

Not knowing exactly who he was, Lyric quickly locked the door, then rolled the window down halfway to get a closer look and to see what he wanted.

"Yo, Lyric, I know you not trying to act like you don't remember me? Did you just lock the door?"

She lifted up her shades trying to distinguish his face. He looked so familiar, but she still didn't know who is was. "Do I know you?"

"Hell, yeah. It's me, Russell, Portia's cousin."

Lyric covered her mouth then rolled the window all the way down. "Russ? Oh my God, you look so different. Portia did mention to me that you might be coming to the wedding, but I wasn't sure if you would make it. Oh, shit. It's been a minute since I've seen you." Even through his khaki suit jacket, she could tell his body was buff just like the rapper, Nelly.

"Yeah, it has," Russell said. He leaned into Lyric's car window giving her a slight hug. "I've been staying with her since I got back in town two days ago. I'm surprised she didn't tell you."

Lyric shook her head back and forth. "Well, I guess she's been so busy with the wedding that she just didn't have time."

"Yeah, that nigga Charles been looking at me sideways ever since he met me," Russell mentioned with a slight laugh. "It's cool though. As long as that muthafucka treat my cousin right, he don't have to like me."

"So, did you see Sheena?" Lyric held a childhood grin.

"Yeah, I peeped her out, but I didn't say anything to her yet. She look good though, just like you."

Lyric blushed a little bit then patted her typical brides-maid's updo hairstyle. "Thanks. I see prison altered your look, too. You got big as shit in there. Plus, you let your hair grow out a little bit. You never kept it curly back in the day. Are you glad to be out?"

"Hell, yeah. Let's go get some food and catch up and I'll tell you all about it. A nigga starving, I ain't ate shit all day. I was surprised as hell that Cuz and her man didn't have no reception. Is that some new shit?"

Lyric laughed then quickly decided to take him up on his offer. She wasn't in the mood to go home to an empty house. Diesel had warned her before she went to the hairdresser early that morning that he would be home late...as usual. Lyric hit the remote to unlock the door and Russell hopped in eye balling her new car as they took off down the street.

"Damn, I see somebody getting paper," Russell said looking around. "This shit still got the new car smell. It's been a minute since I been in a new whip like this." He was overly excited.

Lyric wasn't impressed. "It's okay."

"I hope you got me on this meal because I'm broke as hell," Russell said with a slight laugh. Between the bus ticket from Florida to North Carolina along with some food along the way, he only had fifteen dollars left. Even Portia had been nice enough to buy him the new clothes he wore.

"Yeah, don't worry, boo, I got you."

"I know you didn't buy this shit. What's the niggas's name? Do I know 'em?"

"Look, I'm not trying to talk about him right now," Lyric replied.

A few seconds into the ride, Lyric noticed the Lexus following her again. She knew from time to time the Feds would follow her to try and send Diesel a message, but something felt different this time.

Russell noticed her looking in the rear view mirror and saw that they were being followed. "Take this quick right."

"Onto the highway?" Lyric asked.

"Yeah, not unless you know who the fuck that is. We bout to see how this thing really gets down."

Suddenly, Lyric whipped her Benz to the right and headed down the entrance ramp onto 77 North and gunned her SL as fast as she could make it go, with speeds reaching at least a hundred.

Two exits down, Russell looked back. "See, we smoked that Lexus. You can slow down now."

"This shit is crazy."

"Lyric, I ain't trying to get in your personal business but, who the hell is following you?"

"I don't know. Maybe it's the Feds or the local cops or

something, shit I don't know. It's nothing, I'm not use, to," Lyric responded with a nonchalant attitude.

Russell looked at her wondering why she didn't see anything strange about the whole situation. He made himself a mental note to find out what was really going on. "I doubt if the Feds riding around in a fucking Lexus." He paused for a moment. "Shit, I just got out. I don't need to be fucking with you then." Surprisingly when Russell went to check in with his Parole Officer the day before, he hadn't said a word about the incident with Liyah. It was obvious that she'd taken his advice.

Fifteen minutes later, they pulled up at Tsunami Japanese Steakhouse near Concord Mills after Russell kept talking about fried rice. After finding a parking space right in front of the restaurant, Lyric and Russell headed inside. Luckily, Lyric had left one of her light weight jackets from Arden B inside the car, so she quickly put it on to camouflage the bridesmaid dress. Her look wasn't what she would call a fashion statement, but for now it would have to do. Lyric noticed a female coming out the restaurant eye balling and smiling at Russell, causing him to return the gesture.

"Boy, if I were you I would leave women alone for a while. That shit that went down with your wife is crazy," Lyric mentioned. "What happened with that? I didn't even know that you got married."

Russell stopped in his tracks and frowned. "Don't you dare bring up that bitch."

"Damn...alright. Calm down. Didn't know the subject was so sensitive," Lyric replied.

Moments later, the hostess led them to one of the long tables that sat eight people and handed them both a menu. As soon as they were seated, she asked if they would like a drink while looking over the menu. Russell ordered two rounds of Patron and Lyric ordered a glass of Kendall Jackson, Pinot Noir.

Russell looked around like a kid in a candy store. "Man, I thought you were going to take me to a regular Chinese carry-out or something. I didn't know it would be somewhere fancy like this." He'd never seen a restaurant where they cooked the food directly in front of you." He pointed to the grill. "So, they gonna cook the food right there?"

Lyric smiled, showing her deep dimples. "Yes. I almost forgot that you been locked up for so long. Whatever you order, they are gonna cook it right here."

Seeing places like that, instantly made Russell miss being home. Looking over at Lyric suddenly made him remember a part of his childhood. "It's so hard to come back here and not be able to see Mama Moses. I miss that woman so much. She was more like a mother to me rather than a grandmother," Russell said, making conversation.

"Shoot, I know, I miss her, too. You already know if it weren't for her or Portia, I don't know where I would be right now. We had some good times in that house, didn't we?"

"Yes, we did. We were young and crazy. Time has flown by. It's hard to believe that we're in our thirties. Shit, I'm knocking on forty's door by five years. Do you remember we used to call ourselves the three musketeers?" he asked with a huge smile.

"Hell, yeah. We never missed a party, concert, or a night at Starlight Roller Rink on Harris Boulevard."

"I forgot about that. Me, you and Portia were tight back then." Russell laughed. "I remember you and Portia used to tell people I was y'all bodyguard and shit."

"We gave you that name because you would always cock block on any dude that tried to holla at us."

"That's because those niggas weren't good enough for my girls. Mama Moses used to tell you and Portia, to date doctors or lawyers and leave all those hustlers and shit alone. Then she would send me out to go look for y'all, thinking I was the innocent hard working grandson. Little did she know y'all were dating them hustlers only to get the nigga's info so I could stick their ass up. We hit up half the drug dealers in North Carolina back then.

Lyric shook her head in agreement. "We were all eating

good back then until we put Sheena's stupid-ass on the team. She almost got us all killed trying to set up that nigga from Jersey."

"What's up with Sheena's crazy-ass anyway?"

"I don't know Russ, Sheena off the chain even more so now. She hasn't been right since you broke her heart. She's even into women now. It's all your fault. You turned her out."

"Sheena knew what type of nigga I was from the jump. She bought any heart- ache on herself. That girl has always been a damn freak. Y'all just didn't know about that shit," Russell said with an attitude.

"Whatever, Russ. After she had a daughter we thought she would calm down, but she started wilding out even worst."

Russell looked surprised. "Sheena has a daughter? I didn't know that. How old is she?"

"Dee is sixteen…almost seventeen actually. Other than being a little grown for her age, she's a beautiful girl. Smart, honor-roll student. She had to grow up fast living with Sheena. That's my baby though; my Goddaughter actually. I spoil the shit out of her whenever I get the chance," Lyric bragged. "If it were up to Sheena, she would walk around in Wal-Mart shit, while her ass is rocking Prada. Sheena seems to love her, but Portia and I can't seem to understand why she treats her the way she do. Like she hates to look at her sometimes."

"Sheena got a lot of issues. I can't see her even having a baby. Who's the father?"

Lyric shrugged her shoulders. "Some nigga she met from South Carolina or something like that. We never met him. I think he ended up dying in a car accident." She sighed. "Portia and I helped her get a place and get back on her feet after she had her daughter. I even offered to take the baby so she could focus on herself, but after she saw the money and assistance she could get off her she declined my offer."

"Boy, are you still writing in those notebooks? You used to write in those things all the time," Lyric said.

Russell was surprised. He had no idea that Lyric remembered that about him. "No, not really. I gave that up a while back," he lied. Russell didn't want to let Lyric know that he still had the unusual habit.

When the waitress approached with their drinks, they gave her their orders of Hibachi Steak and Shrimp. After she walked away, Russell looked over noticing Lyric's huge diamond ring.

"So, what's up with you? I see that big-ass rock on your finger. That nigga must love you."

Lyric looked at her finger. "I don't know about that."

"Stop fronting. If a nigga put a rock on your finger like that, he playing for keeps."

When Lyric avoided eye contact, looking around at the other people eating in the restaurant, Russell immediately picked up on it. He could tell she had some heavy shit on her mind. He also remembered overhearing Portia talking to Charles the night he got home about Lyric catching her man in the club with another woman. He wondered if Lyric was still with that same clown he met briefly years ago or if this was another circus act. *If so, he must have stepped his game up,* Russell thought after seeing Lyric's ring and the whip she was driving. He never liked the nigga from day one. Russell had watched Lyric during the wedding ceremony and he could see the pain in her eyes, and deep down, he wanted to make her happy. He'd actually had feelings for her since they were young, but every time he would express himself to her, she always turned him down due to their brother/sister relationship.

"Lyric, can I ask you a question?

She took a sip of her wine. "Yeah, shoot."

"Why do you put up with the bullshit?"

Lyric hesitated before answering. "What the fuck is that supposed to mean, Russ?" She quickly took anther sip.

"Lyric, you're too beautiful to be with any man who won't marry you and keeps cheating on you." When she didn't respond, he continued. "Men will only do to you what you allow them to."

Lyric looked away in a daze, as if she was searching for something else to talk about. The last thing she wanted to do was talk about Diesel.

"You aight, Lyric?" he asked after noticing her blank expression.

Lyric nodded realizing she had to quickly end the subject. "Look Russell, I haven't seen you in what…sixteen years, and you think you know so much about what's going on in my personal life? My life is fine, I ain't never been clueless to the game, trust and believe and I can be married right now if I wanted to."

Russell threw up his hands. "Alright. Whatever. Just know I'm here for you and I'll punish that nigga if he keeps stepping out of line."

Lyric wondered how Russell knew all her business in the first place, but was also touched by his concern. They'd only been together for a few minutes, and he already had one up on Diesel. They glared into each others eyes for a few minutes. "So Dr. Phil, what have you been doing with yourself, since you all up in my damn business? I know you have plenty of women running after you since you came out of prison looking all cut up. You sure don't look like the Russell I used to know." She wanted to change the subject before she really flipped out on him for getting all up in her personal space.

"Well, I had started working out at the gym before I went in anyway. That's when I met that bitch. She was working as a personal trainer there." Russell downed his drink and began to bite his bottom lip. "Yeah…yeah. She was definitely a bitch."

Lyric seemed shocked by his response. "I couldn't believe it when Portia told me you had a wife."

"Yeah, I got married and it was the worst fucking mistake I ever made. I thought she was really the one. That is until I seen some pictures of her in bed with one of my boys. When I went to confront that bitch, she had the nerve to tell me that she was leaving me for another nigga. Like that shit was really gonna go down."

Lyric was almost speechless. "Damn, I'm sorry to hear that."

Russell stood up and removed his suit jacket and laid it over the chair. Lyric glanced down at his shoes at the same time. It wasn't the normal Gucci loafers he used to rock, but she admired how neat he was. Russell had always been fly, which was something Lyric loved about him. She would've probably ended up giving him some back in the day, but Portia constantly told her, he was off limits. Not to mention, Russell always acted a little weird, which turned her off most of the time. Lyric sized him up. *Damn, Russell turned out to be fine.*

After a long meal filled with conversation about their lives, Lyric and Russell both were about to burst. Russell continued the discussion, telling Lyric that once he got back on his feet he wanted to invest some money into a restaurant. Lyric shared her plans of opening her own business as well, something she had never told anyone. After several hours and dirty looks from the staff wondering how long they were going to hold up the table, they finished up with dessert and finally left.

"Where am I taking you? Back to Portia's?" Lyric asked as she pulled out of the restaurant's parking lot.

"Hell, no. That nigga Charles didn't want me staying at their crib while they were on their honeymoon, so that nigga put me up in a hotel until they get back. I can already tell that's he's a petty muthafucka, but I'm trying to keep my cool for Cuz. Otherwise I would've knocked that nerd looking muthafucka out by now."

Lyric smiled. "Yeah, Charles has the tendency to rub people the wrong way. You know how anal some investment bankers are. So, where you staying?"

Russell pulled out a piece of white paper in his pocket. "The Holiday Inn University Park or some shit. They could've at least put me up in the Marriott or something." He sounded ungrateful, but didn't care, especially since it was Charles' money who'd paid for the room.

"Oh, cool. That's about ten minutes from here. Let's head

there now," Lyric suggested. She'd checked her cell phone a few times while in the restaurant to see if Diesel had called to at least ask about the wedding, but as usual there were no missed calls. Ready to curse him out, she wanted to drop Russell off first since he was already in her business earlier.

During the drive, Russell ran his hands across the butta soft leather seats, then across the wood grain. "This car is fly as hell Lyric, the real deal. She got to be worth at least sixty-five thousand. Trust me I used to get Motor Trend magazine while I was locked up, so I know."

"I guess, but who cares how much it costs. I mean don't get me wrong, I love this car. Call it love at first sight. I saw it on the show case floor and had to have it, but I just don't like the way I got it. Every time my dude, Diesel, fucks up, he buys me stuff, thinking that's supposed to make things better, but he has no idea. I'm so over that shit."

"I feel you,' Russell replied, realizing the nigga Diesel was definitely buying Lyric's love and that was probably the reason why she dealt with his shit.

After a brief moment of silence Lyric turned up the radio and they continued reminiscing while listening to Power 98. They sang along with Laurel Hill as her raspy voice bellowed out, "Killing me softly with his words." When they pulled up to the hotel, five minutes later, Russell turned down the music and looked at her.

"I hope you don't think we are finished," he protested. "Come on, let's have a few more drinks for old times."

"Sorry Russ, I'm exhausted," Lyric said yawning." She was faking, but he didn't have to know it.

"Come on. Is there anyway I can persuade you?" he pressed her.

Suddenly, Lyric's phone began to vibrate. Thinking it was Diesel, she almost broke her neck trying to get it out her purse. However, once she looked at the screen, and Sheena's name popped up, Lyric quickly threw the phone back in her purse. *I am not in the mood for her ass*, Lyric thought. She hesitated for a second then agreed. It had been a long time since she'd seen her childhood friend, and was really enjoying his company anyway. Besides, her life revolved around Diesel and she was slowly trying to get her old self back.

Upon entering the hotel, Russell and Lyric went straight to the bar and didn't hesitate ordering drink after drink until Lyric looked down at her Presidential Rolex watch with the diamond bezel, realizing it was almost 12:00 a.m.

"Damn, I know Diesel is blowing me up!" She looked in her clutch bag and checked her cell phone, but the only call she saw was the earlier call from Sheena. She felt relieved and pissed at the same time. "That muthafucka probably up to no good," she said out loud.

Russell smiled. "Who, your man, Diesel?"

Lyric shook her head. "Yeah, fuck him. That nigga ain't called me all day, but I bet when he gets home he gonna want some pussy." She had no problems telling Russell her business now. "The hell with that. I've caught his ass with too many women, so he ain't getting shit from me." She picked up her phone. "You know what…I should call him now."

"Oh, hell no. That's probably what he wants," Russell said, grabbing the phone. "Don't feed into that shit. Let that nigga worry about your whereabouts for a change. It sounds like he got too much power over you."

"Last call!" the bartender yelled.

"Damn, this bar closes early," Lyric stated even though she was already good and tipsy. At that moment, she felt like her bladder was about to burst, so she excused herself and went to the bathroom.

Russell watched as she walked away. His mouth watered as her ass shook with every stride she took. *I'm going to get some of that pussy, by any means necessary*, he thought. When she returned to the table a few minutes later, Russell had ordered her another glass of wine.

Lyric took the drink to the head and got up grabbing her purse and keys.

However, her equilibrium was totally thrown off and she stumbled back, falling into her bar stool. Russell looked around in the bar then at Lyric, "Damn, you still can't handle your liquor. I can't let you drive like this. Come up to my room and drink a cup of coffee, it will make you feel better and then you can be on your way."

After forging Lyric's signature on the credit card bar tab, Russell helped Lyric to her feet. She closed her eyes tightly to keep her head from spinning. All her weight leaned against Russell as they walked toward the elevator. As he held her tight and sniffed her hair, he couldn't believe how good it smelled. Once they were in his hotel room, he sat Lyric down on one of the double beds and took her shoes off before making his way over to the coffee pot.

As Lyric rested her spinning head, she fought to hold her eyes open but was unable to. Suddenly, she thought she felt her legs being spread part, and tried to close them, but couldn't. Moments later, she felt her bridesmaid's dress being pulled upward and her red thong being exposed. As Lyric began to mumble something, it felt like a finger was running along side her pussy, tickling her hairs until suddenly, the feeling stopped.

# Chapter 8

The next day, Lyric was awakened with a pounding headache. She laid in a slump trying to focus, noticing unfamiliar surroundings. When she opened her eyes all the way and realized she was in a hotel room, she quickly sat up. Getting out of the bed, Lyric could feel the soft carpet underneath her tired feet as she tried to pull herself together.

A few seconds later, Russell opened the bathroom door, and walked out wearing a towel around his hips and wiping shaving cream off his face. After a glimpse of his sexy chest and washboard abs, Lyric's eyes lit up.

"Umm…what happened?" she asked "Please don't tell me we did anything." Lyric looked down and noticed that her bridesmaid's dress was still on.

"Oh, no. You had too much to drink last night, that's what happened. I couldn't let you drive, so you crashed out on the other bed," Russell replied. The truth was, he really hadn't done exactly want he wanted. After lifting up her dress, taking off her thongs and running his hand across her pussy, all of a sudden, he stopped. Hearing the voice of Mama Moses telling him to, "Listen and act accordingly," something she said to him and Portia in church all the time; made him stop instantly. If it was one person he listened to, it was his grandmother; the only woman besides Portia who ever loved him unconditionally.

Russell reached in a small travel bag and handed her some Tylenol and a glass of orange juice that sat on a breakfast tray.

"How did you know I had a headache?" Lyric asked.

"An educated guess," Russell said with a smile.

After Lyric took the pills she thought, *How come I can't remember anything? Damn, my head hasn't hurt like this in years.* Looking at the clock that read 9:30 a.m. Lyric went into panic mode. "Shit, I gotta get up outta here. I know Diesel is flipping out!" she said jumping up.

A frown appeared on Russell's face at the mention of Diesel's name.

"So, you caught the nigga with another bitch and now you running home. I never thought you would play yourself like that," Russell said.

Lyric was pissed. "You got some fucking nerve judging me."

As Lyric picked up her clutch and made her way toward the door, Russell stopped her. "I'm sorry, Lyric. I just hate to see you get hurt. It's obvious that you can do better."

Lyric was immune to apologies, but Russell's actually sounded somewhat sincere. "Russ, don't worry about me. I'll be fine. Write down my number, so we can keep in touch," Lyric suggested. She tucked her clutch bag under her arm while carrying her heels in the other.

"Aight, what are those digits?" he asked after grabbing a pen and paper off the desk.

Lyric cut her eye in his direction and quickly blurted out her cell number. When they approached the door, Russell forcefully reached over and gave Lyric a hug pulling her close. Catching her off guard, Lyric shivered as he pressed his warm body against hers. A whirlwind of emotions struck her after feeling his thick body. Embraced in his strong arms, Lyric felt the warmth of his breath as he moved his lips up her neck giving her a kiss on the cheek.

*Damn,* Lyric thought, as her pussy started getting moist.

She could feel a hard erection bulging through the towel that barely covered him. Lyric instantly reflected back to when they were teens and he used to grind up on her during all the school dances. She recalled how big his dick felt back then so she could only image what he was working with now. She pulled from his embrace smiling.

"What are you smiling about?" Russell asked suspiciously.

"Nothing, just thinking," she said, throwing up the peace sign and leaving his room.

Lyric swiftly walked toward the elevator as her heart raced with excitement.
Part of her wanted to run back in Russell's room, rip the towel off and fuck his brains out. Then the other part of her knew if she did, she might regret it later, but she still felt it was something worth exploring.

She pushed the down arrow then glanced in the beautiful brass mirror hanging in the hall. She frowned up her face at the sight of her tired drooping eyes and flat lifeless hair. She reached in her clutch and pulled out her faithful elastic Goody ponytail holder and pulled her long hair back.

She breathed a sigh of relief when the elevator door opened and she was away from Russell. Once the elevator reached the lobby, Lyric noticed a crowd of well-dressed black men gathered near the seating area and ballroom. She'd never seen so many black men together in one place with out some shit jumping off, it was a beautiful thing.

She glanced in the direction of the ballroom and saw a sign that read: Welcome to the 10th Annual Black Lawyer's Convention. *Interesting*, Lyric thought as she proceeded toward the marbled stained front doors. She reached down to put on her Manolo pumps and turned around bumping into a good-looking man.

"Oh, excuse me," Lyric said slightly embarrassed.

"No, excuse me. It's my fault you bumped into me," he said, with a huge smile revealing his pearly white teeth.

"Your fault?" Lyric asked with raised eyebrows.

"When the elevator doors opened and I was embraced by your beauty, I had to rush over and meet you. I was paralyzed and couldn't move out your way."

Lyric hesitated before saying anything. "So, you're a stalker, huh?"

"Let's just say I love beautiful things," he said, extending his hand.
"My name is Maxwell".

Lyric looked into his sexy light brown eyes, "Hello, I'm Lyric," she replied shaking his hand.

"Lyric? That's a beautiful name".

"Thanks, well nice meeting you."

When she turned to walk out the door, Maxwell was right behind her. "Lyric, please take my card and call me sometime. I would really like to take you out. It will be worth your while, trust me."

Lyric didn't want to be rude so she kindly accepted his business card, and said goodbye. While walking to her car she glanced at his card, "Maxwell Tyson, Attorney at Law. He's fine and he got legit money. I need to hold on to this," she said, placing the card in her bag.

Lyric jumped into her car wishing it wasn't such a chilly day. She wanted to ride with the top down so she could clear her head. After quickly pulling out the hotel parking lot, she took a left turn and hit highway 85, speeding. On the way home, Lyric rode in silence. Her mind was all over the place as her Benz glided smoothly down the highway as tears freely flowed down her face. She thought about her mother, something she hadn't done in a long time. She hadn't seen her since she was fourteen years old. Lyric's memories of her were fading now. Not that she had too many good memories to begin with. Her heart still ached when Lyric remembered the day her mother walked out and never came back. Over the years, she often wondered where her mother was or if she were even still alive. She'd even gotten Russell to look for her back in the day, but the lead always came up cold. It was times like these, that Lyric wished she had a father. Someone to run to, cry on his shoulder and have him tell her things would be alright. Lyric then began to think how her mother and father's absence could've possibly made her immune to bad relationships.

Picking up her phone, Lyric dialed Sheena's number then waited for her to answer. When Sheena didn't, Lyric hung up and tried again. "Shit!" Lyric yelled after the third call. Knowing her friend was probably asleep after a long night of hoeing, she ended the call again. "I really need her ass to pick up, so we can get the story straight. I'm just gonna have to tell Diesel that I was with her all night." She dialed the number again, but this time when Sheena didn't answer, Lyric left a message. "Call me asap," she said hanging up. Even though she didn't have any missed calls from Diesel on her cell, she still wanted to be ready just in case.

Lyric soon pulled in her driveway making a thirty-minute trip home in twenty. She turned right into her subdivision. She looked around admiring her neighborhood in South Charlotte, thinking back to a time where she used to be so happy, especially when she and Diesel first moved in. She then began thinking about when the two of them met during Charlotte's first CIAA weekend. As soon as she saw him driving his brand new Bentley with custom rims, Lyric along with several other girls gawking, instantly fell in love with him and the money they knew he had. Not to mention, he was from New York, so that was a plus. However, Lyric outshined them all. After catching up with him at a party, Lyric introduced herself at the bar, and they had a brief conversation, clicking immediately like Khloe Kardashian and Lamar Odom.

Lyric gave him the pussy that same night and the next morning Diesel splurged, taking her on a shopping spree at South Park Mall. Lyric remembered him buying everything she wanted out of Tiffany and Company, Nordstrom's and Neiman Marcus.

Soon after, they were taking trips that included more

shopping sprees, purchasing several his and her mink coats, and matching platinum jewelry. Diesel introduced Lyric to the glamorous life and did everything to capture her heart. However, the true love he once had for her was now gone.

She wiped her tears away and reached above her head and pushed the garage remote. Once the door slowly opened, Lyric was relieved to see Diesel still wasn't home and mad all at the same time. Even though she wasn't in the mood to deal with one of his bullshit interrogations, it still didn't hide the fact that she was pissed about being disrespected once again. She now labeled him a disappointment just like her mother; or her father for that matter.

After pulling inside and cutting the ignition off, Lyric got out the car and closed the garage door before quickly going inside. Pausing on the staircase from the sudden vibration of her cell phone, she answered it even though it was an unknown number.

"Hello."

"Just seeing if you got home safe," Russell replied.

Lyric wasn't use to any man being this thoughtful. "Oh, yeah. I just walked in actually."

"Well, if you can get away sometime tomorrow or next week, call me at the hotel. I enjoyed catching up."

"Sure. I'll call you later," Lyric said. She didn't want this to be a lengthy conversation.

"Cool," Russell said hanging up.

Once Lyric went upstairs, she checked the voicemail on the house phone. The first message was from Diesel.

"Yo', Lyric pick up the damn phone. I know yo' ass is home. Well, check it, I'll be home later. Got some shit to handle, I'll make this all up to you! Real talk."

Lyric hit delete and listened to the next message. It was an old message from her doctor that she'd obviously forgot to check. "Lyric Brody, this is a message from Dr. Gilbert's office reminding you of your doctor's appointment Monday morning."

"Damn, I forgot about my appointment today," Lyric

said. It was time for her yearly pap, and to see if Diesel had given her any new STD's.

Trying to deal with her anger, Lyric started getting undressed and looked down. That's when she noticed her thong was turned inside out. She was puzzled because she always looked at her body from head to toe in her large, expensive, leather cowhide floor mirror before getting dressed. Lyric suddenly came out her daze when she finally heard the loud rap music from Diesel's car entering the garage. She quickly ran and messed up the bed to look like she slept in it, then ran like a track star in the Olympics and jumped in the shower.

# LOVE HEIST

# Chapter 9

Diesel entered the bathroom and removed his clothes; he knew he had a fight on his hands as he watched Lyric through the large glass shower door. He admired her perfect body, and her wet hair flowing down her back. He'd just laid the new chocolate diamond necklace on the bed in hopes that she wouldn't stay mad and let this new episode linger on for weeks like some of his past episodes. Besides, he had plans to go out of town, and didn't need her tripping. After taking off his clothes that actually smelled like his latest victim's pussy, he made his way closer to the shower door then slowly opened it.

"Damn, you shoulda been one of those Sports Illustrated models, baby," Diesel said, as he made his way over to join her. He knew the sweet words weren't going to work, but it still never stopped him from trying.

After stepping inside, he wrapped his arms around Lyric then softly kissed her ear. "Yo' before you get mad, let me explain. I just need to go ahead and tell you that I think I have a problem wit' alcohol. I'm finally admittin' it, baby. I fell asleep in my car this time and…"

Before he could say another word, Lyric quickly turned around to face him, took her fist then punched him in the chest as hard as she could. Diesel had a slim build, so Lyric wasn't afraid of him in the very least. She'd go toe to toe if she had to.

Diesel stumbled backwards against the shower door as Lyric threw several more vicious blows. He wanted so badly to hit her back, but with all the information she knew about his occupation, decisions like that were completely foolish.

Diesel managed to push Lyric away then grabbed onto her, holding her tight. "Please, don't do this. I'm sorry, baby. I'll do whatever I have to in order to make this up to you. Please don't act like this, Ma," he whispered in her ear.

His words were so soothing to her. She loved to make him suffer and that's what she wanted to hear in order to get what she needed from him, which was, enough of his money to leave and still maintain her lifestyle. Lyric tried to continue to fight, but the grip he had on her was too strong.

"Lyric, baby stop!" Diesel yelled this time. "You sitting here trying to fight me, when you know I have a problem. You should be trying to help me." He hoped his sympathy card was working.

Lyric stared at his brown sugar complexion and perfectly shaped goatee. However, she said nothing as she focused on his hands sliding down her wet soapy back then started to finger her from behind. Diesel knew that normally turned her on, so the majority of the time he was in trouble, that's the route he took. It didn't take long for Lyric's breathing to intensify as he leaned in placing his face close to hers. His fingers began to thrust in and out even faster.

Lyric was still mad, but being horny had completely taken control. She whispered in Diesel's ear telling him, "If you keep that shit up, you're going to lose this pussy forever."

"I know, baby. Trust me, I know. Now, turn around and bend over," he demanded.

Lyric looked into his eyes and said, "Talk that shit baby."

She turned around like she was told, placing both her hands against the shower door. Seconds later, Diesel got on his knees, crawled up behind her, then placed his tongue between her ass cheeks. With his tongue now doing the talking, Lyric twitched and moaned yelling out his name.

"Oh my God, that feels so good. I hate you sometimes, you know that?"

"Yeah, baby, but I'm sorry," Diesel said in between licks.

When Lyric couldn't take anymore, he picked her up then carried her dripping body from the shower and into their beautifully decorated master bedroom. Once in the room, he put her down on the chaise lounge and slowly licked and sucked her wet breast like a baby being fed. She braced her body as the chaise lounge rocked back and fourth. Her soaked pussy had sensations running all though her body that sent chills down her spine. At that moment, Lyric pushed Diesel back, dropped to her knees and grabbed his dick, going down on him. It was a risky move since she had no idea who he'd been with, but once Lyric was horny, it was hard to for her to think straight.

He smiled in gratification as she deep throated his dick while holding his balls gently in her hand. Diesels eyes rolled back in his head as he moaned over and over. Lyric sucked him with force, allowing him to make love to her face. He had to admit, no matter how many women he'd fucked, no one could suck his dick like Lyric. She sucked it so good, he often wondered why he even messed around on her at all.

*Maybe it's a sickness*, he thought as Lyric continued to work her magic.

Lyric loved Diesel's thick curved dick. She knew how to stroke it with her hands and mouth sending him into pure ecstasy. Diesel slammed his dick into the back of her throat letting her know he was still in charge. She gagged and her eyes watered, but as usual, she took it like a pro.

Moments later, Diesel lifted her up onto their huge California king-size bed that was adorned with a gorgeous six hundred thread count comforter. He slightly pushed her chest back, parted her legs and placed two fingers inside her treasure. Lyric let out a moan as she enjoyed her man's touch. After a few seconds, he finally pulled out his fingers and Lyric reached down and grabbed them placing them into her mouth. She was definitely freaky in the bedroom.

Lyric sucked her juices off his fingers like candy. Diesel was so anxious; he couldn't take it any longer and slid his manhood inside her dripping wet pussy. She wrapped her legs around his back knowing that drove him crazy. Diesel made love to Lyric in slow motion hitting her g-spot just the way she liked it. A motion that gave her multiple orgasms, as a single tear streamed down her face.

*I'm so weak when it comes to him*, she thought.

After hours of making each other cum, their bodies enjoyed the breeze from the huge ceiling fan as the smell of raw sex now lingered in the air.

Lyric laid motionless thinking, *our make up sex is always so good! Why do we always make the best love when Diesel is in trouble? I wish this man would just do right.*

Diesel also laid in deep thought, his heart pounded as he rubbed her soft skin. He didn't want to keep hurting her either, so he knew he eventually had to do right by her. He tried so hard to stay faithful, but pussy was a man's weakness, especially when it's thrown at you left and right.

Diesel picked the diamond necklace that had fallen on the floor, then propped himself up with one of their huge feather pillows. He turned Lyric's head in his direction before giving her his latest gift.

Lyric studied the two carat necklace that she wasn't crazy about. "Thanks," she said unenthused.

"Lyric, real talk, I know you were pissed about seein' me wit' that bitch at the club that night even though you tried to act like it didn't bother you. But that's just how shit goes in this business. She was new in town and I have money invested wit' some of her peoples. They asked me to show her around town. It was business not pleasure." He pushed some loose hairs out of her face. "I'm out here on the grind makin' a better life for us, so I will be able to really go legit and leave all this behind. I wanna be able to enjoy our life together, and start our family. But until then, its money to be made. You enjoy the lifestyle, so you got to deal wit' the shit that comes along wit it." Lyric never said a word. "Now, I have to go handle some business in Miami, but when I get back we will talk about settin' a weddin' date, real talk, Ma."

Diesel got up and glanced over at Lyric who was actually falling asleep. It was obvious that she'd heard that story on more than enough occasions. "Lyric, get up baby. I need you to take me to the airport."

She opened her eyes. "Airport, for what?"

"See, if you had been awake you woulda heard me. I gotta run to Miami today, and my plane leaves in three hours. I was even talkin' about us finally settin' a weddin' date. You didn't hear that either?"

Lyric shook her head unenthused. "No."

"Well, I did, but we can talk about that later. Please, hurry up and get dressed. I gotta go," he said, dashing into the bathroom. Once inside, Diesel looked at himself in the mirror and said, "I hope I'm tellin' her the truth and won't get cold feet again. This marriage shit is not my thing, but I know shit ain't sweet the way it is either. Lyric is a good girl and I gotta get my act together." He then peeked his head out the bathroom door. "I called you at home last night, and you didn't answer. Where were you?"

"Here. I must didn't hear the phone," Lyric quickly replied. When Diesel went back into the bathroom, Lyric laid on the bed for a minute before mumbling, "I guess I'm suppose to get excited about that bullshit he talking, a wedding date, yeah right! Diesel has told me this same shit so many times before. It's too late now."

Forty minutes later, Lyric ran down the stairs when she heard Diesel impatiently blowing the horn. She was tired as hell from the sex they had and her head was still hurting from all the drinking the night before. After finally making it downstairs, Lyric closed the garage door and walked toward Diesel's

Porsche truck; a Cayenne GTS.

She could tell by his facial expression he was pissed that she took so long to get ready. "Why the fuck is he rushing me? Shit, his flight doesn't leave for another two hours anyway," Lyric said to herself.

"Damn, you the slowest woman I know," Diesel started as soon as she entered the truck.

Lyric took a deep breath trying to ignore him. She knew he was just trying to fuck her day up, making her mad so she wouldn't call checking up on him while he was out of town. She knew how the whole game worked. He continued running his mouth.

"If you plan to be my wife you gonna have to learn to move faster than that. Shit might be poppin' off out here in the streets and I need you to be able to make shit happen. Real talk!"

Lyric bit down on her bottom lip, which was always a reaction when she was pissed. She adjusted her seat, fixed the mirror and pulled out the drive way skidding down the street.

"Now you got a fuckin' attitude, huh? Keep it up, you gonna make me choke the shit out of yo' ass. You drivin' a seventy-two thousand dollar whip, Lyric. Not a fuckin' Hyundai. Stop actin' so childish." He opened up the glove compartment and took out a napkin before wiping off a small finger print on the window. "Drop me by Jabari's crib first. I need him to handle some shit for me while I'm gone."

Lyric grabbed her Chloe sunglasses to shield the bright sun. She then turned up the music ignoring him as the sounds of the old school go-go song, *I Need Money*, by Chuck Brown blasted from his Bose system.

Diesel looked over at her and turned the music down, then got on his cell phone talking business like he always did whenever they were in the car. Twenty minutes later, they pulled up at Jabari's crib. He was Diesel's best friend who'd moved down to Charlotte from New York with him years ago. He lived in a run down house on Freedom Street. Lyric often wondered why he hadn't fixed up his spot, or sold it and moved to a better neighborhood.

When Diesel got out the car and went to knock on the door, Lyric glanced over at Jabari once he stood in the doorway. He stood, 6'8' with green eyes, a pecan complexion, and a nice build. Out of all Diesel's friends, he was the only one Lyric liked. Obviously raised from a good home, he was a really nice person; a characteristic she wished Diesel had.

She let out a sigh of irritation when she saw Diesel headed back to the car a few minutes later. Once inside, he leaned over and kissed Lyric on the cheek. "You pissed at me, huh? I'm sorry baby for yellin' at you, but you know how I get. I'm an impatient-ass nigga."

Lyric didn't respond. She was use to Diesel's stubborn, arrogant ways, usually followed by one of his temper tantrums. When things between them were good, they were good and when things were bad, they were bad. Diesel grabbed her face turning it in his direction.

"You love me?" he asked in a sexy voice.

"You get on my damn nerves majority of the time."

"That's not what the fuck I asked you, I said do you love me?"

Lyric wasn't in the mood and knew he wasn't gonna let up until she responded the correct way. "Yes, Diesel!" she yelled.

"That's what I thought," he said, kissing her again.

Struggling to hide her disappointment, Lyric gave him a sarcastic smile then pouted her glossy, pink lips. She was beyond sick of his ass on the real.

# Chapter 10

Hours later, Lyric finally reached home after what seemed like forever from dropping Diesel off and going to her doctor's appointment. Finally, she was STD clear... for the moment, which was exciting news. Lyric was irritated from sitting in traffic and took off her clothes and climbed into bed, completely worn out. She tossed and turned, with so many thoughts about her and Diesel's relationship in her mind; a relationship that she eventually had to walk out on. She remembered how she used to miss Diesel so much when he was gone. Now his absence was so routine, it didn't bother her as much. Lately, she'd actually started enjoying the piece and quiet, and used that time to focus on herself.

Lyric grabbed the picture of her and Diesel off the night-stand. She admired how fly they looked while vacationing at The Atlantis in the Bahamas. Just like the song by Mary J. Blige, she reminisced on the love they once had.

Diesel was dressed in white linen shorts and a wife beater looking fine as hell, especially the way all his tattoos popped out on his arms. They'd definitely had some good times, but unfortunately the bad now outweighed the good. At first Lyric played her role as wifey, she dealt with his infidelity as long as he didn't give her any diseases and continued to take care of home, but now even that had changed. She'd become insecure and had let Diesel change her from the confident woman Mama Moses raised her to be. Her mental foundation was now shaky. Mostly due to constant chipping away of her soul by Diesel, his other women, and all the other chaos that seemed to follow him. She felt different, she felt changed, but she wasn't sure if it was for the better or worse.

Lyric jumped out the bed when she heard her doorbell ringing. Almost instantly, the ringing became loud, hard knocks. She threw on her robe and flew down the long spiral stair case to see who was knocking on her door so loudly. They didn't normally get visitors so she hoped it was Jabari and not the police.

When Lyric peeped out the living room window and saw some girl with two little girls by her side, she frowned. "Who in the hell is that?" Lyric quickly walked to the door and opened it. "Yes, can I help you?"

"Excuse me, are you Lyric?

"Why? Who wants to know?"

"Well, my name is Sasha and these are my daughters…Diesel's daughters. I think we need to talk."

Lyric slowly backed up, hoping she'd misunderstood what she just heard. She had a look that could kill. "How do you know my name and where we live?"

"Can we come in?" Sasha asked.

"Come in," Lyric said nonchalantly, never taking her eyes off the twin girls.
They looked to be about two years old, with long, curly pony tails. They were dressed in cute matching outfits and shoes. Lyric then eyed the girl who had a cute spiky haircut. She also eyed her blue skinny leg jeans, a cute off the shoulder shirt and the latest Jimmy Choo paisley stud bag; a bag that Lyric hadn't even had the chance to get. "So, what's up?" Lyric asked the petite woman.

"Look Lyric, I went into The Galleria Hair Salon about

two months ago to see about buying the shop since it's up for sale, and the stylist started talking when I mentioned who my man was. Actually, the entire shop went crazy. They were quick to tell me about you and after some time I found out where you lived. I followed both of you around at first, but then I finally decided to pay Diesel's other women a visit. "

"Diesel's other woman? I'm the main woman, honey. You're actually the *other woman*," Lyric fired back. She knew Sasha was telling the truth because the more she looked at the twins, the more she realized they were the spitting image of Diesel. It was no denying it, even if he wanted to.

Sasha smacked her lips. "Well, that doesn't even matter now because we're both getting played."

"So, you're the one in the green Lexus?"

Sasha nodded her head. "Yeah. The Lexus that he just bought for me once I told him I was getting ready to leave his ass. Shit, he's the reason why I was in the salon in the first place. He offered to buy it for me. He wanted me to move back to Charlotte so he could be closer to the girls."

"Yeah, I get my hair done there almost every week, so they know me well," Lyric replied in a state of shock.

"After I found out your name, I asked him about you, but he denied it of course," Sasha mentioned.

Sasha went on to tell Lyric that she'd met Diesel in the strip club where she was working at to pay her way through school. They hit it off and he put her up in a condo in Raleigh, which explained why they'd never ran into each other. Sasha also said that after getting pregnant, Diesel had been taking care of them every since. He'd even been staying with her at least once a week recently.

After Lyric listened to Sasha, it felt like now her life was really in shambles, and for the first time she felt threatened. Lyric had to take a seat. The news had cut her…deep. The fact that Diesel was cheating with Sasha didn't bother her so much, but the fact that he was spending that type of money on another bitch, and had two daughters was devastating. She couldn't even have children now because of him. She knew it was really over and she would never be able to forgive Diesel for this one.

Lyric flashed her engagement ring, which meant nothing to her now. It almost blinded Sasha when she caught her peeping at it. While sitting in the living room, Sasha looked around admiring the Italian leather furniture and white Persian rug.

The two continued talking and comparing notes until the conversation was interrupted when both turned to look at the sixty-five inch Sony plasma hanging on the wall. The reality show, Cheaters was coming on.

Sasha gave a fake smirk. "One of us should call that show and bust Diesel's cheating ass."

Lyric rolled her eyes not thinking it was funny and got up leaving the room to call Diesel and do her own version of Cheaters by putting him on blast. "I know I promised Portia I wouldn't react to anything he does anymore, but this shit is an emergency. I have to call him. I can't let this one go," Lyric said to herself. She looked at the time, realizing that Diesel should've landed by now.

She grabbed the cordless phone and hit speed dial, then put the phone on speaker before placing it down on the table.

"Yo, what up Lyric?" Diesel asked, answering the phone with the once hot song, *In Da Club* by 50 Cent blasting in the background.

"Does the name Sasha sound familiar to you?"

Before she could finish her sentence, she looked up and noticed Sasha standing beside her anxious to see what Diesel had to say.

"No, why?" he asked.

Lyric gave Sasha a "See he ain't shit look" before continuing, "Diesel, don't fucking lie. I got a call today from someone telling me that you're the father of twin girls." Lyric's voice went from soft to loud and defensive.

He turned the music down and his voice sounded serious. "Lyric baby, I really don't have time for this. You know I'm takin' care of some business right now. How many times do we have to go over this shit? I don't have any kids. You already know how these bitches lie and try to come at you wit' all kinds of bullshit. We'll talk when I get home, real talk," he replied with an irritated tone.

Lyric looked at Sasha and she could see the steam coming off the top of her head, and the tears building up in her eyes. One of Diesel's daughters heard his voice on the speakerphone and yelled, "Daddy!"

Diesel was speechless for a second, realizing Sasha was there with Lyric. He went into rage mode and flipped the script, yelling in the phone. "I know that bitch aint in our crib. Sasha, you already knew I had a fuckin' girl. I can't believe you disrespected my shit!"

Sasha picked up the cordless phone and started screaming in the receiver. "Diesel, you're a lying bastard. When I asked your ass about Lyric, you said she was your ex and you only still dealt with her because she knew a lot of your personal business and you couldn't afford to cut her off right now. You looked me in my eyes with a straight face. You can deny me, but now you denying the girls? That's the type of shit we on Diesel?"

Diesel was quiet for once.

"If it's the last thing I do, you gone get yours! My brother is gonna get at you. Diesel, you know what's coming, right? The Bloods nigga!" Sasha yelled in a raspy voice.

"Bitch, aint nobody scared of your punk-ass wanna be gang-banging brother," Diesel said, before slamming the phone down.

Lyric grabbed the phone from Sasha, and hung it back on the charger. After the whole ordeal was over Sasha paused to gather her thoughts

"Look Lyric, I don't have a beef with you. He's all yours now, if you can keep his ass alive!"

Lyric jumped up quickly and proceeded over to Sasha. "Keep him alive? Let me give you a word of advice. I've never known Diesel to be a punk so your threats probably meant nothing. If anything you only made him even more pissed off." Lyric didn't want to seem as if she was protecting Diesel because that really wasn't the case. "This is too much for me to handle right now, so please get the fuck out my house!" she ordered.

"What?" Sasha asked.

"You heard me, get out!" Lyric said. She walked to the front door and opened it.

Sasha abruptly grabbed both of the well mannered little girl's arms and walked out looking at Lyric like she wanted to say something else but didn't.

Lyric slammed the door so hard one of the pictures fell off the wall. She watched as Sasha put both of her daughters in the back seat of the infamous Lexus and pulled off. She knew it wasn't Sasha's fault that this had happened, but Lyric was still hurt. She began pacing the floor, telling herself Diesel had finally gone to far. Her days of sitting at home worried about where he was or who he was with were over. Reality was closing in around her.

For the first time in her life, she knew she could make it on her own. The question was how was she going to leave Diesel and still maintain her life style? Lyric planned to make sure she got hers. She had been planning for sometime how to steal Diesel's stash money and make it look like a robbery.

Access to that kind of money would keep her in the lifestyle to which she'd become accustomed to. Hell, she earned it. Unbeknownst to Diesel, she had plans to open up her own business. She always dreamed of owning her own clothing boutique called Fetish. An upscale classy joint that would carry all of the top designer clothing, shoes and handbags. Fashion was her true gift.

Lyric had even found the perfect spot while she and Diesel were out shopping in Los Angles a few months ago. While Diesel was asleep in the hotel, Lyric managed to slip away and meet with the management company, secretly inquiring about the property. She was glad that she'd stashed away a couple of dollars here and there from the money Diesel had given her over the years, which allowed her to be able to afford the $3,500.00 a month rent until business picked up. Now all she had to do was move out there and get started, and if everything went as planned she would have it, courtesy of Diesel.

"He's gonna hate that he ever fucked me over," Lyric said, before going back upstairs.

# LOVE HEIST

# Chapter 11

While driving the newly rented Dodge Charger to meet his boy, Ski, at a nearby sports bar, Russell tapped the wheel to the beat of Trey Songz and Drake's song, *Successful*. It felt great to be out of prison, and he couldn't wait until he became successful. He constantly thanked Portia out loud for secretly leaving him some money before she left like she was sitting in the passenger's seat. Russell knew that once he got back on top, she would be the first person he hooked up. As he continued down Tryon Street, Russell looked over at a nearby bus stop and noticed a woman who resembled his dead wife.

"What the fuck," he said trying to get a slower look. "It can't be." He quickly pulled over to make sure as the voices returned.

*"There's that bitch. Get her ass for trying to leave you,"* the voices said. This time they were even louder than before. *Get her now before it's too late.*

Not giving it a second thought, Russell floored the gas pedal, driving his car up onto the sidewalk toward the woman yelling "Bitch, why are you following me. I'll get rid of your ass for sure this time!"

As soon as she heard the tires squeal, the woman jumped out of the way without a second's notice as Russell tried to run her over with his car. She ran for her life and ducked inside a nail salon just in time. Hearing her screams of horror instantly caused Russell to snap out it and quickly pull off the curb. Speeding down the street like a professional driver, Russell continued to hear the voices, while he continuously hit his head. He yelled back, "Shut the hell up, stop talking to me...stop talking to me!"

At that moment, Russell began to think about his prescription from Dr. O'Malley and wondered if he should at least take a pill every now and then. He knew Lyric would never be with him if she ever found out about his illness. "Maybe I'll think about getting the pills if this shit keeps happening. I mean, I don't really need 'em, but they might calm me down," Russell said, trying to convince himself.

Several minutes later, Russell pulled up at Bikinis Sports Bar for the meeting. He was feeling edgy and needed a damn drink. "I hope I don't have to fuck nobody up in this muthafucka," Russell mumbled as he walked inside the bar. The foul odor of stale cigarettes, buffalo wing sauce, and cheap liquor hit him dead in the face.

The place was crowded, which instantly made Russell feel a little nervous as he made his way past the various flat screen televisions. Crowds of people always made him hallucinate and feel like everybody was watching him. However, the waitresses walking around in tiny bathing suit tops made him feel a little better.

"I almost forgot how fine white girls can be," Russell said, looking at one blonde girl in particular. "She's at least a 36 C." He then bumped into a cutie almost making her spill her drink. "Oh, I'm sorry."

She smiled at him. "No problem, good looking. I'm sure you wouldn't mind buying me another one if you did spill it."

"No doubt. What's your name, gorgeous?"

"Diva," the attractive female replied.

"Interesting name," Russell said. "Actually take this for your troubles since you're so damn sexy." Russell handed her a ten dollar bill like he was paid. He then looked into her sexy hazel eyes that reminded him of his mother's.

*Calm down, she's not your mother*, Russell told himself over and over. He wasn't trying to have another episode.

Diva smiled again. "Thanks big spender. I'm sure I'll see you around."

"I'm sure you will, too."

Just as Russell was about to turn around, Diva grabbed his arm. "Here's my number, just in case you ever wanna have some fun."

*Damn, bitches were never this easy before I got locked up.* "Cool. I'll make sure I use this," Russell replied before walking off. He wanted to stay and rap to her a little more, but at the moment, the meeting with his friend was much more important than pussy.

Russell walked off scanning the smoke filled room and spotting his friend, Ski sitting in the back near the pool tables. Russell was shocked to see he wasn't alone. When he reached the table, Ski didn't waste any time giving him a hard pound and a hug.

"My man. You look good, bro," Ski said.

"Thanks, man," Russell replied.

When Ski noticed Russell looking at the other men, he made the introduction, "Russell this is my crew, Dread and Pretty Boy Mike. This is my old partner I was telling you about, Russ."

Russell was pissed. Not only did Ski fail to mention anything about the other two men over the phone the day before, but he didn't trust a lot of people and he damn sure didn't like them knowing anything about him. He glanced over, mugging each one of them. He had to see what type of niggas Ski hung with.

*Fucking with a lot of niggas will get you jammed up. I don't like working with no crew. I can always rely on myself to get in and out in record time. Plus it's too many hands to have to feed later*, Russell thought to himself.

Dread was a heavy set dude with long dread locks. He looked like he was from up top, maybe Jersey. *I can always spot a Jersey nigga. They have a certain swagger about them,* Russell thought as he eyed him. Pretty Boy Mike looked like a pretty Al B. Sure type nigga, dressed in a plaid Polo shirt and some long cargo shorts. By looking at him Russell couldn't figure out where he was from, but wondered what the fuck he was doing at the meeting at all. He looked soft. Russell immediately felt uneasy but sat down to at least hear Ski out.

He was focused on getting that money, and not the minimum wage paying kind. That's why when Ski mentioned a small portion of the plan over the phone, Russell immediately agreed to meet him. Whoever the nigga was, Ski said he was loaded and Russell wanted in. He was itching to get at another nigga. Little did they know, Russell would cut throat all of them. All he needed was a little info on the target.

"Listen up," Ski said, over the loud music. "From what my reliable sources told me, who happens to be a bitch I fucked a couple of times, she said this nigga name Remo is loaded with at least a hundred thousand stashed up in his crib. He owns three barber shops around town, but you know how the nigga got the money to start them muthafuckas." No one said anything as Ski continued. "From hustling of course. The nigga still slinging. She said he's not one of them partying types though. He's laid back and likes to chill at the crib or take one of his many women out. This makes him even easier to get at."

Russell had heard enough, he wasn't good at listening to others. He cut in, taking over the conversation. "How long you been watching this nigga, Ski?"

"About a month," Ski answered,

"That's too long, within two weeks you should know all you need to know about a nigga. If you keep waiting, then he might slip away. We should be hitting his ass up soon. Like I always say, there's no time like the present," Russell said, looking around the table to read everyone's face.

Dread looked over at Ski. "Yo, who the fuck this new nigga think he is?"

*Up north niggas always act like they run shit,* Russell

thought.

"Yeah, we got this, just slow your role and follow our lead player," Pretty Boy Mike agreed.

"Chill the fuck out, listen to what the man has to say!" Ski yelled. "Trust me, this man knows what he's talking about. I told you, he's my old partner."

Russell's facial expression immediately changed. Rage came across his entire body. He shook his head from side to side when he started hearing voices again.

*That nigga trying to play you dog.* Russell tried to block it out. The voices kept repeating the same thing in his head. *That nigga trying to play you. That nigga trying to play you!* The voices said even louder.

Russell walked over to one of the pool tables, and grabbed a pool stick, which happened to be laying across the green felt. Moments later, he walked back to the table, holding the stick over his shoulder like he was going to bat at a baseball game. "Say another muthafucking word."

Dread looked as if he was getting ready to reach for a gun under his crisp Polo shirt.

"Go head, reach for it, nigga, I dare you!" Russell yelled. At that point, a few people started to look in their direction. "Don't ever disrespect me like that, nigga. You don't know me."

Ski stood up and looked at Dread. "I told your dumb-ass before he got here, that this man was a loose cannon."

"Fuck you and that crazy-looking nigga," Dread replied. "Y'all do this shit by yourselves then." He stood and headed for the door.

Pretty Boy Mike decided to follow his friend, but quickly turned back around. "Ski, I might still be in man, so call me later."

"As long as your ass is a solider and not a pussy, we might call," Russell said speaking up for Ski. Russell then watched as Dread and Mike slowly walked outside and hopped into a beat up Cadillac.

After they left the table, Russell finally sat back down

and placed the pool stick across his lap. "Now…Ski, you want to get this money or what? Let's get down to business." He then laid down how he thought the heist should go down.

Ski was all ears since he had just finished doing a bid and his robbing skills were a little rusty compared to the shit Russell was talking about doing.

After several hours of plotting, planning, and drinking, Russell and Ski were up to speed on how everything would go down. Depending on the situation, Pretty Boy Mike was to stay in the car as a lookout while Ski and Russell went up after the nigga and put that fire to his ass. Dread was completely out the picture. Russell refused to work with him anymore, and Ski was about that paper so he didn't mind him being out.

After a couple shots of Vodka, Russell got up to leave the bar. His eyes were drawn to a woman wearing a short black skirt leaning over the pool table as she hit the eight ball into the corner pocket. The lights were dim, but he could see the crowd of gorgeous females gathered in the corner cheering the cutie wit the booty on as she leaned over for another shot.

"Damn, she got a phat ass," Russell said. He was just about to make his way over toward the crowd when he realized he left his brand new Yankees fitted hat at the table. He doubled back, got his hat, pulled it down low like Jay-Z and headed over to the pool table to introduce himself.

"I'm gonna punish that pussy tonight, if she doesn't want to give it up, I'll make her," Russell said. He remembered how back in the day he would get women so drunk that they would pass out, which instantly gave him permission to rape them. They often woke up not knowing what happened, allowing him to get away with each incident. Russell knew now that people used date rape drugs to assist with sexual assault, and in his mind, he had to get his hands on some of it.

As he made his way over, he could tell she had just won the game, when he saw her grab the money off the pool table and stick it in her bra.

"She's sexy, too," Russell mumbled as he continued

watching her from the back. She threw her long hair for side to side.

The smoke stained mirrors in the pool area gave the beautiful bombshell a view of what looked like the silhouette of a fine built physique headed in her direction. She squinted her eyes to see if she knew him, but the lighting from the chandelier was too dim.

She started gathering all the balls to rack up for another game as Russell walked up closely behind her. He leaned over her shoulder whispered in her ear.

"Can I have next?"

Never answering him, she moved her plump ass back up against him and leaned over to grab a ball out the corner pocket. This gave Russell the green light.

"Better yet, let's leave this spot and get to know each other better," he suggested.

She quickly turned her body around looking at the tattoo on his neck that read: King

"Hummmm…King, I'm feeling that name. I'm Pam, let's get up outta here!"

In the wee hours of the morning, Russell opened his eyes in shock and stumbled from the bed and onto his feet. There was blood everywhere and furniture was thrown all over his hotel room. He looked down at his torn t-shirt which was covered in blood. He quickly removed it and checked his body for wounds, but didn't see anything other than a few scratches. He then noticed his bruised and swollen knuckles.

"Where the hell did all this blood come from?" Russell wondered. He stepped over some couch pillows searching the room and saw several empty bottles of cheap champagne and broken glasses on the floor. That's when he noticed that one of the champagne glasses had a light pink shade of lipstick on it.

Russell rubbed his hands across his head and sat down

on the bed that had been stripped down to the bare mattress. The sheets were now in the corner of the room.

"What the fuck happened?" His head pounded as he tried to remember. He quickly jumped up off the bed when he heard a slight moaning sound coming from the bathroom. When he eased over to the door and peeped in, Russell saw a naked female body hunched over in a fetal position inside the bathtub.

"Oh, shit." Russell had immediately remembered her from the sports bar. Her honey-blonde weave and bright green finger nails jogged his memory. "But how did she get in my damn room? Did I fuck her up like this?" he wondered.

Pam opened one of her swollen bloody eyes, and instantly started screaming when she saw Russell walking toward her. As Russell put his hand over her mouth, she started shaking, holding up her hands up as if she thought he was going to strike her again.

"Shhhhhh," Russell told her before removing his hand.

"Please don't beat me anymore. Let me go. I won't tell anybody. I have two kids at home," she pleaded in a low soft tone.

"Relax, I'm not going to hurt you," Russell assured, quickly thinking of a plan. "My twin brother must've done this shit to you. He called and asked me to come over here. He must've had too much to drink and you did something to trigger him."

She didn't respond but continued to cry as Russell picked her up. He then closed the toilet seat and sat her down. Russell took a wash cloth and tried to wipe some of the blood off her face and arms. After cleaning her up the best he could, Russell carried her out the bathroom and over to the bed.

He looked around the room for her clothes and found them on the floor along with her shoes and purse. He opened her purse and glanced at her ID just in case she didn't want to keep her mouth closed.

After helping her get dressed, Russell sat down staring at her as she sat in a complete daze. "Listen Pam, I don't know what the hell happened here, but like I said, my brother must've lost it. He's really not a bad dude, he just flips out sometimes. I promise, I'll make sure he gives you a little something to help you forget this shit ever happened. We have your name and address from your driver's license so it would be your best bet to cooperate. Trust me, your bruises will heal."

Pam looked up at Russell, thinking in her line of work, getting her ass kicked was something she was use to. But she was no damn fool. Even though the room was dark, she knew the man sitting beside her was the same man who'd beat the shit out of her. She also remembered when she called him Daddy, and he instantly flipped out.

"Are you going to cooperate or what, bitch? I gotta go find my brother and fix this mess."

Pam looked at him as if she was looking into his soul. "I won't say a word," she mumbled. She went into her purse and pulled out a pair of shades in the attempt to cover her swollen eyes. Although, it didn't cover the rest of her badly beaten face. "Can I go now? I really need to get home to my kids."

"Sure," Russell replied.

When Pam slowly got up and walked out the door, Russell walked behind her and watched her limp slowly down the hall to the elevator never looking back at him.

Walking back into his room, he saw a housecleaning cart in the hallway, and reached over to grab a few extra towels and cleaning supplies. After that, he closed the door and quickly started cleaning the room so he could get the fuck up outta there just in case that bitch decided to call the police. It was something about the look she put on that gave him the impression that he hadn't seen the last of her.

# Chapter 12

The luxury Grand Wilea resort where Portia and Charles were staying in Hawaii was unmatched in beauty and serenity. Nestled within forty landscaped acres and steps away from the manicured beach, the five star hotel provided the perfect honeymoon setting. Portia sat in her white two-piece bathing suit, wearing her new Louis Vuitton sunglasses, compliments of Lyric as one of her bridal shower gifts. She enjoyed the sunny afternoon in the secluded gazebo overlooking the warm clear turquoise ocean, beautiful white sand and swaying palm trees. She sipped on her favorite drink, a Fire Island cocktail which consisted of vodka, raspberry juice and coke.

She remembered the first time she'd tried that drink, it was years back when she, Lyric, Sheena and Russell were partying in Jamaica after robbing a local drug dealer for lots of money. She smiled, thinking back on how much fun they used to have. Portia hated that she didn't get to spend a lot of time with Russell before she left. She missed him so much while he was gone, and hoped that prison had calmed his violent streak. In her opinion, he really was a good guy. People just didn't seem to understand him at times.

At that moment, Portia looked over her shoulder toward the hotel for any sign of Charles. "He's probably still sleeping after the way I put it on him last night," Portia said to herself. She started smiling then suddenly frowned. "But shit, I wish he'd done the same thing for me. Damn, I can't wait until Charles knows how to work this pussy. I'm tired of using my bullet after he falls asleep."

After thinking about their boring sex life for a few more minutes, Portia reached on the small cedar table inside the gazebo, grabbed her cell phone and dialed Lyric's number. After a long pause it went straight to voice mail. "Lyric, it's me, Portia. Please give me call. I've been trying to reach you for two days now. Charles and I are going on a kayak tour in a few minutes, so if I don't answer just leave me a message. I'm just calling to check up on you and Russ. Love you and miss you girl, hope everything is alright." Portia hung up the phone with a bad feeling that something was wrong. She'd tried calling Lyric a few times since she she'd been away, but was unable to reach her.

Portia was just about to dial Sheena to see if she had spoken with Lyric when Charles walked up with a huge smile. "Hello, Mrs. Edwards," he said, kissing her forehead. He sat down beside his new wife on the narrow lounge chair, lifted the towel Portia had over her legs, and snuggled close to her.

"Wow, it's a beautiful day for the kayak tour." When Charles didn't get a response he put his hand under Portia's chin and lifted her head. "What's wrong beautiful? You look like you lost your best friend."

"I can't reach Lyric, and my gut feeling tells me something is wrong."

Charles tried to hold back his disappointment. He did everything he knew how to make their honeymoon the best and all Portia did was whine about her ghetto friends.
"Well baby, I'm sure Lyric is okay. You said she was having some problems with ahhh, what's his name?"

"Diesel. Charles, why can't you seem to remember his name?"

"Yes, Diesel, maybe they took a trip and are trying to work things out and be alone like we are. I'm sure if anything was wrong, loud mouth Sheena would've called you by now."

"Stop calling her that, Charles. That's true, though. I guess

I've been protecting Lyric for so long, the minute I don't hear from her, I think something is wrong."

"It's time you take care of your husband now, she has a man."

"Yeah, you're right."

"Actually, I need you right now, back in the bed." Charles stood up and extended his hand.

"What about the kayak thing?" Portia asked as Charles pulled her to her feet.

"Don't worry about that. We'll reschedule."

Charles and Portia walked hand and hand back to their thousand dollar a night villa. When Charles wrapped his arms around Portia's shoulder, she suddenly decided he was right. She'd been trying to tell Lyric and Sheena for awhile now it was time to grow up, settle down and stop all the fighting. And after what happened the night of her bachorette party, she realized they weren't on the same page anymore. She wanted to build a life with Charles, have kids and enjoy a normal, drama free life.

After walking into their luxury accommodations, Charles picked Portia up and carried her to the bed. "Relax baby I'll be right back, I have a surprise for you," he said, disappearing into the bathroom.

Portia laid back on the bed wondering what her husband had up his sleeve. She hoped it was something that could spice up their sex life. She decided to turn on some music to set the mood. She was so glad she bought her Ipod and Bose speaker along on the trip.

"Are you ready, baby?" Charles yelled from the bathroom.

"Bring it on daddy!" Portia yelled back, teasing him.

When Charles walked out of the bathroom, Portia immediately sat up on the bed and couldn't believe her eyes. He was wearing a black bra, black thongs and a pair of fish net stockings and heels.

Portia was in complete shock "Charles, what the fuck are you doing?"

"What, you don't like it?" Charles asked, dancing around.

"Hell no, what's wrong with you? Please don't tell me that you're gay or some shit and now you're deciding to come out the damn closet."

"No, baby, I'm not gay. My colleagues said they dress in their wives underwear from time to time because it adds spice to their sex life and they love it. That's why I decided to do it."

"Well, they must be some perverted mutherfuckers! Take that shit off now or I'll be getting a fucking annulment." Portia looked down. "And I know those aren't my new Christian Louboutin knotted pumps that Lyric just bought me? Take 'em off. You're stretching them out of place! Are you crazy?" Charles lowered his head with an embarrassed expression, then slid everything off one by one. "Do you need to go to therapy for this bullshit?

"Wait a minute, you're taking this out of context, it was just a joke," Charles tried to convince.

"Fuck that, I don't find it funny at all," Portia shot back with an attitude.

"Portia I've never heard you talk like this before. You sound like your ghetto-ass friends now."

"Well, I never knew you wanted to dress up like a damn sissy either."

Instead of Charles getting pissed off, he smiled. "Actually, talking like this is starting to turn me on," Charles said, turning Portia over. After pulling off her bathing suit, he forcefully entered her, penetrating her pussy hard and deep from behind.

Portia braced herself against the headboard of the bed. Each thrust was pure pleasure as Portia wondered how wearing some women's panties could finally bring out a side of Charles she'd never seen before.

*Oh my God, finally*, Portia thought as her eyes rolled back into her head. "Yeah, baby, fuck me harder," she said, as Charles stroked her at full speed. His heavy breathing and moaning turned Portia on even more. She then screamed loudly as Charles hit her G-spot. It wasn't long before she finally released the best orgasm she'd ever felt.

Suddenly, she felt him jerk then moan her name. "Porti-aaaaaaaaa, I love you!"

Seconds later, Charles pulled out and fell on the bed out of breath with his limp, dripping dick lying on his thigh. Portia slid over beside him, pulling the covers over their naked bodies.

*Damn, I guess I underestimated my husband, but then again I really hope his ass was just joking about that cross-dressing shit,* Portia thought.

# LOVE HEIST

# Chapter 13

After getting out of bed, Lyric finally cut the ringers to her cell phone and all the house phones back on. Diesel had been calling non-stop all night, but she refused to answer. Even though she was tempted to hear what he had to say, she still didn't see the point. There was nothing he could say to make things right. She wasn't interested in hearing another lie. She was planning to make him suffer once and for all. Just like R. Kelly said, when a woman's fed up there's nothing anyone could do about it. It was finally time to get the money she needed to bounce on his ass.

After taking a nice hot shower, Lyric looked in the closet for something to wear. She threw on her "Fuck it all look," which consisted of an over-sized pink and gold Juicy Couture t-shirt, a pair of black leggings and some Tory Burch ballerina shoes. She decided to go on her usual weekly shopping spree. Shopping always made her feel better, helping her forget her problems, but this time she had an agenda…to spend as much as Diesel's money as she could. Without contemplating for even a second, Lyric went straight to one of the stashes Diesel kept in a shoe box inside his custom built closet, and got out three stacks of bills; stacks that were a thousand dollars a piece.

"This should be enough for now. If not, I'll come back

and get more," she told herself.

After grabbing her purse and going downstairs, Lyric entered the garage and immediately walked up to Diesel's black S550 Mercedes Benz that he rarely drove. She would've chosen the Maserati, but Lyric hadn't seen it much since she'd scratched it up. It was even weird how Diesel had yet to question her about the incident. As Lyric hit the button to unlock the door, she smiled.

"He's going to be pissed." She knew Diesel never allowed her to drive his cars unless he was with her. "Yeah, I'm going to dog the shit out of this car. Hell, I might wreck it just to have some get back."

She reached in her pocket and grabbed her cell phone and powered it back on noticing a missed call from Sheena, but didn't bother calling her back.

*She hasn't bothered to return any of my calls, so fuck the selfish bitch,* Lyric thought.

With the news about Diesel's daughters, Lyric wasn't in the mood to be alone, but dealing with Sheena wasn't an option at the moment. Since Portia was still on her honeymoon she had to settle for hanging out by herself.

Suddenly, Lyric's phone vibrated. She glanced at the caller ID. It was Russell. She was curious to see what he wanted.

"Hey Russ," she said answering his call.

"What's up?" he said, smiling from ear to ear. He felt good every time he heard her voice.

"Nothing much, just pulling out my garage."

"You must be on your way to meet me for breakfast?" Russell asked with confidence.

Silence filled the phone. Lyric didn't have an appetite, but she actually wanted to see him. She wondered if being with another man would help get her mind off of the drama with Diesel. Besides, she needed to be around somebody who'd been in her corner since they were young.

"Where you at?" Lyric asked

"At Eddie's Place Restaurant in Ballantyne."

"Oh, alight. That's in my neck of the woods. I'm on my way," Lyric replied. "I guess since it's you, I can postpone shopping for a minute."

She hung up, made a U-turn and drove toward Toringdon Street.

Lyric turned up her Beyonce CD when she heard her song playing; she sang along, like bad karaoke. "Now, now, now, diva is a female version of a hustla, of a hustla, of a hustla." She smiled thinking that the song was going to be her new anthem.

Ten minutes later, Lyric pulled up at Eddie's Place and entered the restaurant. Her model walk drew lots of attention as she made her way toward Russell who was sitting at a table in the back of the restaurant. She could smell his cologne as she got closer. *Damn, he smells good,* she thought taking a seat.

"What are you wearing? You smell really good," Lyric stated. She didn't even bother to say hello.

Russell stood up, greeting her with a hug and a wet kiss on the cheek. "It's some shit called Unforgivable by that nigga Puff Daddy. I stole it from Charles before they rolled out," he admitted. "This is his too, but the shit is a little too tight for me," he said, pulling on the white Lacoste shirt. "Man shit has changed since I been in prison. Rappers didn't have cologne back in the day."

Russell's eyes stayed glued to Lyric as she displayed a huge smile. "Yeah, that shirt does look a little young."

"Don't worry, boo because I got something lined up, that's gonna have me back in business."

By the look in his eyes, Lyric could tell that whatever it was, Russell was up to no good. She wondered if he was back to his old ways. Lyric also remembered when she and Portia used to help him set up and rob dudes back in the day. It was a crazy, yet true bond that they all shared together; a bond that lasted five years until one day, Russell just disappeared. The next thing Lyric knew, Russell had gotten locked up at the age of nineteen for killing his so called wife.

*No, he can't be up to anything. He wouldn't be that dumb. He just got out of prison*, Lyric tried to convince herself. *Then again, Russell is crazy. I wouldn't put it past him.* Suddenly, a light bulb went off. Lyric thought, *that's it, I'll get Russell to help me with my plan. I can tell he's still digging on me and just like when we were young, I can get him to do whatever I ask.*

Russell licked his lips and complimented Lyric, which brought her out of her thoughts. "You look good as shit today. I could eat your ass up right about now."

She smiled thinking of her fantasy about Russell, *he better stop saying that, I just might take him up on his offer.* Her smile grew wider. She was surprised and turned on at the same by his directness.

At that moment, the waitress came over and asked if they were ready to order. The smell of the food lingering in the restaurant suddenly made Lyric develop an appetite. "Yes, I'll have pancakes, scrambled eggs with cheese, and sausage," Lyric said. Russell ordered the same.

After a few seconds of sitting at the table staring at one another speechless, Lyric asked, "So, what you got planned for tomorrow?"

Russell knew exactly what he had planned, but didn't feel comfortable with getting Lyric involved. "A few things. Why, what's up?"

"I wanted us to fly to Vegas for a couple of days, gamble, get our party on, and do it up like we did back in the day. That's if you can get away," Lyric replied with a smirk. "I don't know how that parole shit works."

"Vegas?"

"Yeah, Vegas, trust me it's just what you need," Lyric assured him. *Actually Vegas is the perfect spot to work my magic on him.* Lyric loved Vegas, the shopping, the casinos, and the clubs. The men often lost their minds when they saw her walk in the casinos looking sexy and sit down at the black jack table.

The club, Pure, inside Caesar's Palace was her favorite. It was always jumping and maybe on this trip she could actually dance. She loved to dance, but going to the club with Diesel consisted of sitting in VIP sipping on Moet and Cristal all damn night.

"Can you go out of town yet?" she inquired.

"Man, I don't give a shit about no parole. It's just that, I gotta do something with my man tomorrow. What about Wednesday? Can we roll out then?"

"Sure. I'll hook everything up. All expenses paid on me of course." She knew the last minute plane tickets were going to be outrageous, but could care less.

Russell smiled. "You mean all the expenses will be paid from that nigga you deal with."

"Yeah, so what? Fuck him," Lyric snapped.

"Calm down. Shit, if you don't care about the nigga, I don't either. I don't want you to be with that muthafucka anyway."

Lyric displayed a slight grin. "Why? You want me to be with you?"

"Damn right. I been wanting you to be with me since we were teenagers, but you wouldn't give me a chance. I'm gonna get you sooner or later though."

*This is going to be easier than I thought*, Lyric thought. "Well, you never know what might happen then. We're a lot older now."

Russell smiled. "And that's what I want to hear."

After leaving the restaurant, Russell jumped into his rental car. While driving back to his hotel, his mind drifted to how bad he wanted to be with Lyric. After living in the same house with her and Lyric teasing him with her naked body every once in a while, Russell often got the impression that he would be Lyric's first, but he was wrong. She ended up losing her virginity to one of his best friends and never gave him the time of day, which hurt him…bad.

From that point on, Russell often fantasized about raping Lyric just like a lot of his other women. He would visualize giving her way too much alcohol and then wait until the drug took its affect. Once she was out cold, he would take all her clothes off, make his way downtown and eat her pussy like he hadn't had a meal in days. He would then explore her body, sticking his fingers inside of her vagina, moving them in and out until she was soaking wet. From there he would see him himself pulling out his dick and then ramming it inside until he finally busted a nut.

When Russell stopped daydreaming and approached a traffic light, his dick was hard as a brick. He'd always been obsessed with Lyric, which drove him crazy. His ex wife even favored Lyric, so when she told him about another man, it instantly reminded Russell of how Lyric rejected him, which ultimately triggered something inside his mind.

When he saw Lyric at the wedding, Russell realized that this time, he had to have her. It was reassurance that all he needed was Lyric in his life and all that mental illness bullshit would disappear. However, he also knew that this time rejection wouldn't be an option.

# Chapter 14

Russell walked out of his hotel and onto the busy street waiting for his boy Ski to pick him up. He woke up feeling good. Sometimes waking up was like trying to crawl out of a black hole, feeling detached from his own body. But today was different. Surprisingly, he hadn't had a psychotic episode and his dead wife hadn't shown up as of yet. He still wasn't use to being a free man and got nervous being around a lot of people. Never the less, it felt good to be able to walk outside whenever he wanted to without the permission from someone else.

Looking down at his outdated tennis shoes, Russell realized that he really needed some new gear. After seeing Portia and Lyric's lifestyles, he knew he had to get his paper back up. He loved to dress and after visiting a few of his favorite stores, window shopping wasn't something he was use to doing. As a part of his parole, he'd even applied to several restaurants around town for a chef position, but was getting frustrated when everyone told him they would call when something became available.

"Fuck them people. I can't depend on anybody else. I gotta get this paper, so I can open up my own fucking restaurant.

And if I gotta become the grimy ass nigga I used to be in order to get back on my feet, so be it," Russell said to himself. He got hyped the more he thought about what was about to go down.

Moments later, Russell saw Ski pulling up and he moved back from the curb to avoid getting hit. Ski couldn't drive worth shit. After looking into the car, Russell didn't see the dude Mike, who was supposed to be doing the heist with them. He didn't ask any questions either.

"Fuck it, more money for me," Russell said, jumping inside.

"What up Russ? It's about to go down, baby," Ski said, passing Russell a gun. My girl called and said the nigga Remo on his way to The Capital Grill. We can follow him from there."

"Okay, hopefully this is the night he finally leads us to his crib. This nigga got so many bitches he never goes home," Russell said, putting the gun in his pants.
"Did you pick up the things I told you we needed?"

"Yeah I got it. It's all in the duffle bag in the back seat. Duck tape, rope, extra bullets, gloves, and the ski masks. I'm not new to this, I'm true to this," Ski said, giving Russell a pound.

"We'll see, nigga."

Ski smoked a blunt all the way to North Tyron Street, often asking Russell if he wanted a hit, but Russell faithfully declined. No matter what, he always stayed focused while on a job, and even though he hadn't done a hit in sixteen years, Russell didn't plan on breaking his ritual.

"There go the spot right there, park across the street," Russell stated. "I'm going inside and use the bathroom to make sure he's in the restaurant."

Ski blew a puff of smoke in the air, then pulled over. "Good idea. Make sure he is alone, too. That nigga might've rolled with an entourage tonight."

"I'm on it." Russell said, jumping out the car. After checking his surroundings, he quickly walked across the street.

When Russell retuned a few minutes later, Ski was

smoking another blunt, and bobbing his head to Young Money's song, *Every Girl*. He began to rap as Russell jumped in and closed the door.

Russell disregarded his non-rapping friend. "Yeah, he's in there sitting at the table with a bad bitch. I didn't see any of his boys. Looks like him and the bitch were celebrating something. Pull down the street just in case he saw me."

For the next hour, Russell and Ski sat outside the restaurant waiting for the dude to finish eating.

Ski turned down the music. "Yo, Russ, I never asked you what happened to make you get that long-ass bid in prison."

"Man, I'm not here to discuss my past. I'm trying to look toward the future, and get this paper." Russell refused to go into any details about his business, especially details about his wife. He hated talking about her.

"Yeah, I feel you man. Guess who I saw the other day? Sheena, nigga. Remember how bad she was? Well, all the stripping and tricking has taken its toll on that bitch. Not too long ago me and some of my boys were at The Onyx making it rain on them bitches. Sheena came over and offered me and my boy some pussy for a small fee. You know Sheena got a phat ass, so we of course agreed. She led us to a back room in the club and we both fucked the shit out of her stank-ass. Word around town is that she and her daughter are real freaks."

Russell ignored him. He didn't want to have anything else to do with Sheena and planned to stay the fuck away from her ass. A few seconds later, Russell spotted his payday when he saw Remo staggering out the restaurant. "Get down. There's the target," Russell instructed as he and Ski quickly slouched down in their seats.

As Remo walked past the car with the girl on his arm, Russell eyeballed what looked like an iced out Breitling watch that he knew was worth about fifteen thousand along with a bracelet with just as much bling. They watched as the guy got into the passenger seat and the female jumped into the driver's seat.

"Yeah, we gotta get that nigga!" Russell yelled as he sat back up.

Ski agreed as he started up the car and followed the white Ferrari Spider with 22" inch Ashanti wheels. "That nigga is definitely caked up."

The girl drove recklessly for almost two and a half hours running off the highway, almost crashing the expensive car several times with Russell and Ski hot on the trail.

After driving that long, they soon realized that they were headed to Durham, better known as The Bull City.

"No wonder I ain't never really seen that nigga around town. He lives in Durham. He must just come to Charlotte to check on the barbershops and his bitches," Ski advised.

Ten minutes later, they finally pulled into a subdivision that had a sophisticated yet relaxed atmosphere called Bright Leaf. Russell advised Ski to stay back a few feet so their cover wouldn't be blown. After the car turned right, they proceeded down the street behind them, then finally pulled over and watched as the Ferrari pulled into the driveway of a grand façade brick style home with a two car garage. They sat for a few seconds as the garage slowly opened and the Ferrari pulled inside. It wasn't long before the girl got out, along with Remo and headed inside the house. Remo was obviously so drunk he even forgot to put the garage door back down.

"Oh shit. This is gonna be easier than I thought," Russell said, as he grabbed the duffle bag from the back seat, then slid on his ski mask.

Ski followed his lead. They then checked the neighborhood to make sure everything was clear before jumping out the car. They ran across the street and ducked inside the open garage undetected. After noticing Ski standing in the light, Russell motioned for him to stay down low in a dark corner.

*This muthafucka is back to amateur status*, Russell thought.

After several seconds, Remo surprisingly came back to the garage to get something out the car. He leaned inside still stumbling over his own feet, never noticing Russell and Ski hiding in the corner. Once he stood back up, he looked straight into the barrel of a black Glock 31 pistol. "What the fuck is this? Who the fuck are you? Do you know who you dealing with?" Remo asked. He seemed to sober up instantly.

"Yeah, a stupid muthafucka who just got caught slipping. Where is the girl?" Russell asked.

"She's in the shower," Remo reluctantly replied. "Don't hurt her, man."

Russell threw Ski the duffle bag. "Go tie that bitch up!" Ski grabbed the bag and went inside the house after the girl. "Where the money at?" Russell questioned.

"What money? Everything I got legit, you think I keep money in my crib?"

"Stop lying, nigga. My man saw you last week hit a nigga off with a key of dope and then saw him hand you something in a brown paper bag that look like money," Russell informed.

"What are you talking about? I just own a few barber shops. What…you some dirty police officer or something?"

"Naw, but if I have to ask you one more time where the money is, I'm gonna shoot your bitch-ass."

"I told you before aint no money here," Remo nervously replied.

All of a sudden, a loud shot was heard causing Remo to bend over. "One shot to the shoulder. The next shot will be in your muthafuckin head!" Russell yelled.

Remo leaned back on his car holding his shoulder in pain. "Shit!"

Russell walked up on him putting the gun to his head, "If I don't get what I came for…"

"Hold up, man. I got a couple of dollars in my safe in the guest room upstairs."

"That's what I thought. Lead the way," Russell said, pushing the gun in his back as they walked inside the house.

The extremely spacious four bedroom home was extravagant. The living room had high vaulted ceilings, European furniture, a 50'inch plasma on the wall and a hundred and fifty gallon saltwater hexagon fish tank.

Ski was in the large first floor master suite tying up the girl, who'd been pulled out the shower. "Please don't kill me!" she begged and pleaded. "I'll do whatever you want!" Her voice was loud and squeaky and irritating the fuck out of Ski. He grabbed a sock and stuffed it in her mouth, then ducked taped it shut.

When Russell walked past the kitchen he almost lost his mind. It had hardwood floors, cherry wood cabinets, an island in the middle of the floor with granite counter tops, and stainless steel appliances. The double DeLonghi stainless steel extra large ovens were his favorite.

*Damn, I could cook some serious shit in this kitchen,"* Russell thought. He pictured himself making a serious meal with Lyric sitting on the counter drinking a glass of wine.

Russell, with his gun still planted in Remo's back, waited for Ski to finish before the three men went upstairs to retrieve the money from the safe. They followed Remo into the guest room, where he instantly went to the closet where the safe was located. After dropping to one knee, he played with the safe's dial a few minutes, acting like he couldn't remember the code.

At that moment, Russell hit Remo with the butt of the gun, causing blood to spatter from his fore head.

"Don't play, muthafucka. Punch in the code!"

Not trying the same dumb act twice, Remo wiped the drops of blood as they fell in his eyes, then quickly punched the code to the safe. After opening it, he quickly gave them all the money.

"How much?" Russell asked. When Remo didn't reply he got louder. "How much?"

"About fifty thousand," Remo responded.

Russell looked disappointed. "Where's the rest?"

"Come on, let's get the fuck outta here," Ski said to Russell. "We got everything that was in the safe."

However, Russell wasn't satisfied. He knew it was more money in the house. He could feel it. "Get the fuck up!" he ordered Remo.

As they all walked back downstairs, Russell started scoping out Remo's crib a bit more. Seconds later, he walked over to the large book shelf in the living room. Something about it didn't look right. He studied it for a few minutes and cut his eye in Remo's direction.

"What the fuck you looking at some books for nigga, we already got the money.
Let's go," Ski said getting impatient.

Russell tuned Ski out, still watching Remo's reaction as he started moving some of the books of the shelf tossing them on the floor. Remo looked away and mumbled something under his breath with a funny expression on his face. That to Russell, was an indication that Remo was hiding something and he was close to finding out what is was.

Russell started tossing all the books off the shelf until he came across another safe planted inside the wall. "Bingo, whatcha got here? You holding out?" Ski ran over after realizing Russell had found another safe. "What the fuck you come running over here for now? Your ass wanted to leave before!"

"Man, chill out," Ski said, moving closer to see the safe.

Still bleeding, barely able to stand, Remo said "Come on man. You got what you want, just go head."

"Go head?" Russell asked, walking up on him smacking him in the face with the butt of the gun again. "If you don't get over there and open that damn safe, I'll kill you and your fucking girl."

Remo stumbled over slowly opening the safe and pulled out several wads of cash. It appeared to be at least sixty thousand. Ski reached over grabbing the money as Russell loaded the bag. Russell could see the terror in Remo's face wondering if they were going to kill him or not.

"Lucky for you, I got what I want. See you on the next come up," Russell said tying Remo to a chair.

# LOVE HEIST

Right before leaving, Russell grabbed the watch and the bracelet Remo wore from earlier, then grabbed the bags and quickly ran out the garage door with Ski not far behind. Moments later, they jumped in Ski's Chevy Malibu and pulled off.

Russell scanned the neighborhood, wondering if anyone had heard the gunshot.

"Let's get the fuck outta here before one of these neighbors calls the cops and we both violate our parole. I don't know about you, but I'm never going back to that shit hole."

# Chapter 15

After the robbery, Russell and Ski hit 85 South headed back to Charlotte.

Ski was so hyped up from the big score he talked continually. "Russ, how did you know that nigga was holding out and had another safe in the house?" Ski asked.

"It's called skills nigga, I'm not new to this…I'm true to this," Russell said, with a huge smirk on his face.

"This shit reminds me of back in the day when we used to put in work," Ski continued. "Man I missed this shit."

"Yeah, I missed it, too. It feels good to have some fuckin' paper again."

After riding for about forty five minutes, Ski saw the sign for Greensboro. "Hey Russ let's stop in Greensboro and hit up the strip club, Sugar Bears. We need to celebrate our score, and what better way than to watch some asses clap."

Russell smiled from ear to ear. "Sounds like a plan to me. I haven't been to a real strip club in years." He was ready to slap some ass.

Ski took the Farragut Street exit heading for the strip club and within twenty minutes they were pulling into the parking lot. From the outside, the place wasn't all that. It had a gravel parking lot, and put you in the mind of the strip club in the movie, *The Players Club*. They even had a small stature guy standing outside, working the door as well. Russell couldn't wait to see if the owner of the club looked liked Bernie Mac's character, Dollar Bill.

When Russell and Ski got out and headed toward the door, the short guy eyeballed them before frisking them down. "Welcome to Sugar Bears, fella's. Hope you enjoy," he said, opening the door.

After nodding their heads, Russell and Ski walked inside and headed straight for the bar. It was a packed house and Russell could smell pussy and sweat all throughout the club. The bright red walls made the club seem large although it was tiny. Russell appreciated the fact that it was relatively clean on the inside, which meant the owner probably cared about the way his girls looked. The last thing he wanted to do at the moment was give his money to some ole dirty bitch. However, when Russell finally saw some of the dancers scattered around the club, he knew his theory was completely wrong. Not only did they look dirty, but in his opinion, most of them needed to find some other way to make money. They weren't attractive at all and certainly didn't look like his baby, Lyric.

He glanced at a few of the tables that had some baller nigga's holding up several wads of cash in the air. Even though he and Ski were there to celebrate, Russell had already made up his mind that if he caught one of them dudes slipping, they were going back to Charlotte with two hits in a night.

"Damn, she needs some ass to be working in here, right?" Ski inquired as he pointed to a thin, shapeless stripper that reminded both of them of Kelly Rowland. She was on stage finishing up her routine.

"Yeah, that bitch don't have a body, but she cute as hell in the face," Russell replied as the girl picked up the few bills she had on the stage and left. "She might wanna get some of that plastic surgery shit if this is going to be her career."

"Let me get a Henney and Coke," Ski said to the overweight bartender. "What you drinking, Russ?"

"Nothing actually."

"Aww, come on man. We here to celebrate. Why you playing me like that?"

"Nigga, I ain't playing you. I just don't wanna drink. I'm gonna celebrate by looking at some tits and ass and possibly giving these bitches some good tips. Besides, I need to be focused." Russell didn't want to tell his friend that alcohol might really get his voices all riled up.

"Man, why you need to be focused now? The job is done," Ski announced.

"I'm alright. You just do you. Don't worry about me," Russell advised.

A few seconds later they heard the DJ say, "Get your money ready for the baddest bitch in the Carolinas, back by popular demand...It's Candy!"

The place went crazy. Dudes started standing up cheering and whistling. Pushing and shoving trying to get to the front of the stage.

"Damn, she must be good," Russell said to Ski.

"Who, Candy? Man that bitch is the shit. She can make a two liter soda disappear in her pussy. I seen it for myself when she came to Club Onyx in Charlotte, and she fine with a bad-ass body."

"Well, if that's the case, I need to see too." Russell moved closer to the stage to get a better view. He had to see this girl. Seconds later, he watched as Candy came out and danced to the center of the stage shaking her ass to, *My Goodies*, by Petey Pablo and Ciara.

She was wearing nothing but a tiny green g-string that was hidden deep in her ass, and a diamond studded bikini top. Her tight abs, tiny waist, and thick shapely legs mesmerized the crowd as she jumped on the stripper pole and did a back bend, sliding down the pole with her legs draped around it.

When Russell's eyes bulged, Ski hit him on the shoulder. "I told you that bitch was bad!"

The crowd cheered and threw several one dollar bills all

over the stage. After walking across the stage seductively on her hands and knees like a cheetah, Candy laid on her back, spread her legs and grinded her pussy in the air. Moments later, she managed to make eye contact with Russell, who stood close to the stage. While all the other dudes was making it rain with dollar bills, Russell pulled out a hundred dollar bill and waived it back and forth. It didn't take Candy long at all to roll over and grab the hundred dollar bill from his hand. She stood up, danced in front of him then stuck her hands inside her pussy. After licking her finger one by one, Russell handed her another hundred dollar bill. Teasing him even more, Candy blew him a kiss, grabbed his hand and placed it on her plump ass.

"Slap that ass!" Ski yelled overly excited.

*Fuck slapping her ass, I need to be fucking her right now*, Russell thought.

Even though it was against the rules, Candy jumped off the stage and made her way up to Russell. It wasn't long before she turned around, sat on his lap and began giving him the ultimate lap dance. Grinding her ass on him in a slow circular motion made Russell's dick hard within seconds. Candy definitely knew what she was doing, and had all the other men in the club, wishing they were Russell.

She leaned back and rested on Russell's chest. "You like it?"

Russell wanted to place his finger inside her pussy so bad, but knew the bouncers would kick him out. They were already looking like they wanted to stop their little show. "Hell, yeah."

After sitting back up, Candy continued to grind, but then stopped once she looked toward the door. She seemed startled as she quickly hopped back on stage and made her way back toward the pole. Wanting to see what had her spooked, Russell turned around and saw some dude in a red Black Label shirt come in with an entourage of about six other guys.

All of a sudden the music went down. "Let me give a shout out to Face and the crew…Greensboro's finest. The real money niggas are in the house!" the DJ announced.

The owner instantly ran out of the back and made some people get up and cleared a table right by the stage for Face and his crew. Moments later, one of the waitresses ran over to their table with three bottles of Moet.

Russell had to laugh. He turned to Ski. "Real money niggas, huh? Well, we'll see about that."

When the music went back up, Russell started feeding Candy even more hundred dollar bills as she continued to dance. Even though she seemed a bit distracted now, she still tried her best to entertain the crowd.

Face frowned up when he noticed Russell paying extra special attention to his girl. It didn't take long for him to send one of his boys over to tell Russell to move. The biggest dude in the crew walked up on Russell with a fake gangster attitude.

"Yo, Face said move from in front of his girl, you blocking his view of her performance."

Russell turned and looked at Face. Looking like Lil' Wayne with his diamond grill, Face smiled, held up a bottle of Moet then gave Russell a head nod.

"You alright, Russ?" Ski asked, looking the big dude up and down. He was ready for whatever.

"Damn, right," Russell replied. He looked at the big guy like he was only five feet tall. "Fuck you and your man over there, I'll move when I'm finished watching the show," Russell said, turning away. He eyed the empty Heineken beer bottle sitting on the table next to him.

The big dude looked at Face and gave him a look. When Face nodded his head like he was giving some type of approval, the big guy instantly grabbed Russell from behind. However, Russell was on point. He reached for the beer bottle and cracked the big guy across the head. *The bigger they are the harder they fall,* Russell thought when he saw the dude stumble back. Trying to finish him off, Russell punched the giant right in the middle of his neck and watched him finally hit the floor.

"Here they come," Ski said as the rest of the entourage

started coming their way with guns in their hands. Several shots were fired into the air causing the crowd to instantly scream and scatter.

Hating the fact that him and Ski had left their guns in the car, Russell ran and jumped on the stage trying to escape through the back, but security grabbed him first.

"What the fuck you grabbing me for? Those niggas are the ones with the guns!" Russell shouted.

It seemed to take forever before the rest of security was able to get the crowd under control then escort Face and his crew out. Even though they didn't want to leave, out of respect for the owner, they finally jumped in Face's black Denali and left. Minutes later, security escorted Russell to the door and tossed him and Ski out the club. Russell started pacing back in fourth, as the voices in his head were telling him, "Its time for war. Get your gun out the car. Go find them niggas!"

"Russell man, let's get up out of here. We don't need this type of heat right now. Trust me, I want to get them niggas, too. We can sneak back up here at a later date and hit 'em hard. But right now, we got all this money, and don't need the police rolling up on us."

Russell thought about what Ski said. "Yeah, you right lets roll, but be on the lookout for them muthafuckas just in case."

When they got in the car and pulled out the parking lot, Russell looked at the sign that read, Sugar Bears. He had plans of coming back to this spot. Being disrespected was something he never tolerated.

An hour later, the two were back in Charlotte splitting the money in Russell's hotel room. After Ski left, Russell grabbed his things and jumped in his rental, headed uptown to another hotel. He realized he'd broken the number one rule, letting Ski come to his spot.

"When you doing dirt, never let anyone know where you lay your head," he said to himself. "Not even your partner." He smiled thinking about all the money he had. He was ready to hit the town for some long overdue splurging, but just enough not to draw any unwanted attention. "Lyric will be all on a nigga now once she sees that the old Russell is back!"

# LOVE HEIST

# Chapter 16

Lyric headed to South Park Mall after deciding to postpone her shopping spree for one day. After meeting Russell for breakfast, she'd decided to treat herself to a spa day instead. As stressed out as Lyric was, shopping could wait, pampering on the other hand couldn't. Now, even though the circumstances regarding her life was completely jacked up, she felt good, relieved, and on a mission.

"I got to get some sexy shit to have Russell eating out the palms of my hands," Lyric told herself. "I don't wanna give him any chances to tell me no." She nodded her head to the old school rap song by Jay-Z and Foxy Brown, "Aint no nigga like the one I got. No one I can fuck me better. Sleeps around but he give me a lot." Lyric began to laugh. "I can understand exactly where Foxy is coming from," she said, singing along with the hook.

After parking her car, Lyric hadn't even stepped out before she heard Sheena's daughter, Diva yelling out her name then quickly sashayed over toward her. Diva was cute, smart and sexy. She had the prettiest walnut colored complexion and nice curly hair; hair that didn't need a perm every six weeks. To Lyric, Diva didn't look like Sheena so she assumed she looked like the guy from South Carolina; a guy she'd never seen. She was sixteen going on thirty and most men thought she was a grown woman because of her womanly body. With 36 C breasts, small waist, and an ass like the rapper, Trina, nothing about her said sixteen.

However, Diva was definitely out there, which had Lyric worried about her Goddaughter getting hurt or pregnant. Looking at Diva's, cute cropped-style jacket that stopped at her waist, made Lyric remember Sheena mentioning how Diva and her girls had older men buying them all kinds of designer shit. It bothered Lyric that Sheena encouraged Diva's lifestyle at such a young age and she worried that Diva was following right in her mother's footsteps.

"Hey, Auntie Lyric. Where you been, I miss you," Diva said, leaning her head in the window and glancing over in the passenger seat. "And I'm feeling that Gucci bag. That's the new Boston bag that just came out. I saw it online. It's hot," she said reaching over giving Lyric a hug. "When can I borrow it?"

"Dee, you know I got you. I just got a lot of money from Diesel, so I might get you one today," Lyric advised. She hated calling Diva by her real name. She thought it was beyond ghetto and wondered what Sheena was thinking when she named her that. "But don't let me see none of your friends rocking it like you did with that Fendi bag I got you a few months ago." Lyric looked over in the direction of Diva's hot-ass friends.

"Oh, my fault, Kim just wanted to borrow it for that one night."

"Um huh, you know I spoil only you. The rest of them little tricks gotta get their own shit. I told you, wait until you get ready to go to college, I'm going have you so fly, them chicks on campus gonna be hating on you so harddddd!"

Diva smiled from ear to ear. "Aight, I like the sound of that. Whose car is this? I've never seen you drive it before."

"It's Diesel's."

"Oh, that asshole let you drive his car. Wow, what's wrong with him?"

"Watch your mouth," Lyric warned. *Even though you're*

*right*.

Lyric had love for Diva. She was the daughter she wished she could have one day.

They both looked across the street when they heard hissing sounds coming from the brake pads of the city bus pulling up at the bus stop. "Can I go with you Lyric?" Diva asked pouting her lips. "I don't wanna ride the bus home."

"Sure."

Diva didn't waste anytime waving good bye to her friends as Lyric got out the car and headed toward the entrance of the mall. Minutes later, the two headed straight for Lyric's favorite stores like Louis Vuitton, Neiman Marcus and Nordstrom purchasing something for them both in every store. Diva watched in amazement noticing that Lyric was on a first name basis with almost every sales person.

"Damn, I shoulda got more money," Lyric said as she stepped out of the Apple Store with all her bags."

"Thanks for the IPod Touch," Diva said. "I've wanted one for a while."

"No problem. I wanna roll past Diamond's Direct before we leave this area. I need some new jewels to rock with the rest of my shit," Lyric mentioned. It was her all time favorite spot and the manager was Diesel's boy. Not to mention, Lyric was their number one customer.

After jumping back into her car, and driving to the store, which wasn't located very far from the mall, Lyric received the royal treatment as soon as she parked in front and walked inside.

"Hello, Ms. Lyric. What can we do for you today?" the manager asked, walking over and grabbing her hand to kiss it. He looked just like Christopher from the TV show, *The Soprano's*. He was a cutie and such a damn flirt.

"Hey, Kevin," Lyric said, removing her hand from his grip. "What you got new up in here?"

"I got something just for you, just came in today, but I thought you were here to pick up the pieces Diesel ordered for you about two weeks ago," Kevin replied with a huge smile.

Lyric wondered if the pieces were really for her or for another bitch, but it didn't matter. Whatever it was, the shit was going home with her. "Oh, yeah that's right. I almost forgot." Lyric watched him go in the back to the large safe in the wall then return shortly with a large box. When he opened it, Lyric's eyes lit up. It was an iced out diamond bangle with matching earrings. "Damn."

"Beautiful, huh? The bracelet is five carats and the earrings are three. I thought you knew about this stuff. One of my employees said you came to pick it out with him," Kevin announced.

Now Lyric knew the jewelry really wasn't for her. "Yeah, like I said. I forgot all about it. Go ahead and wrap it up, Kevin." She then wondered if the jewelry was for Sasha.

"Tell Diesel to come see me. I have some new pieces in that he might like. He will certainly turn some heads with this stuff," Kevin said, after placing the fine jewelry inside a bag.

*Something else to draw more bitches*, Lyric thought to herself.

Lyric grabbed the bag. "Alight, I'll definitely tell him to give you a call," she said, with a fake smile. When Lyric peeped Diva winking her eye at some guy in the store, she grabbed her Goddaughter by the arm and pulled her outside. "Girl, stop that shit. That man old enough to be your grandfather," Lyric said, shaking her head. *Like mother like daughter*, Lyric thought.

When Lyric got back to the car she began to massage her temples once a slight headache emerged. No matter how much she was use to it, the fact that Diesel was taking care of another women, bothered her every time.

*I wonder how many more babies Diesel got out there,* she thought to herself.

"Auntie Lyric, are you okay?" Diva asked.

Realizing her mind was in another place she turned to focus on Diva. It was also bothering her that she was more than likely sleeping around with older men, and Lyric hoped she was smart enough not to get caught out there.

"Dee, I'm worried about you. I heard about all this shit these men are buying you, and I don't like it. It's all part of the game, trust me I've been there. It's a high that you can't come down off until it's too late. Most of these hustlers are just looking for a naive young girl to hold their work, put houses and cars in their names, and when shit gets hot, leave their asses to hold the charge for them," Lyric said, hoping to get through to her.

"I know Sheena is going around telling lies on me." Diva never called Sheena, mother. "She's always in my business and got something to say about everything I do. She's never interested in my grades, how well I'm doing in school, or coming to any of my award programs. But the minute she see me with some new clothes, she wants to be all up in it trying to see how I'm getting it so she can get a piece of the pie." Diva wanted to tell Lyric about her mother sleeping with Diesel so bad, but remembered what Diesel had warned her about. Even though she and her mother didn't really get along, Diva didn't want to see her get hurt either.

Lyric nodded her head because she knew that Diva was telling the truth. "So, why are you dating these guys? You shouldn't be worried about that. All you need to focus on right now is school."

"I mean, the guys aren't that old, Lyric. Some are four years older than me, others are a little older, but age doesn't even matter. As long as they treat me good, what difference does it make? As long as I'm not dumb enough to get pregnant like Sheena did, then I don't see the problem. Hell, what can I do? These men come after me, most of the time." Diva didn't want to lie to Lyric entirely. The men did treat her well, but most of the time she didn't force them to wear condoms. Also, she and her friends normally sought after older men just so they could be their sugar daddies.

"Who cares what they do for you? It's still not right, Dee," Lyric said. "I need you to slow down with that shit."

"Trust me, it's not that bad, but okay. Anything for you,"

Diva replied. However, little did Lyric know, Diva had plans on contacting the guy she'd bumped into at the bar the other night. It was something about him that was intriguing. "Well, I'm not even gonna lie to you. You might end up seeing me with this cutie I met at the Bikinis Sports Bar the other night. He was fine. I gave him my number, so hopefully he'll call me."

Lyric was beyond frustrated. "You have to be twenty-one to get up in a sports bar. How do you and your hot-ass friends always get in there?"

"Kim messes with one of the bouncer's at that particular bar, and he slides us right in," Diva stated proudly.

"What's this dude's name and how old is he?"

"I didn't catch his name, and I'm not sure about his age yet, but trust me he didn't look that old. Maybe he's young like me." Diva smiled, but Lyric didn't. "For some reason I don't think he hustles because he only gave me ten dollars when he almost spilled my drink, so that's probably a good thing, right?" Diva tried her best to play with Lyric's intelligence.

Lyric shook her head back and forth realizing that nothing she said was getting through. *She might just have to learn the hard way.*

❤❤❤❤❤❤

Lyric walked up to Sheena's door and noticed two motorcycles parked on the side of the house. One of which was her cousin Kendra's. She caught an instant attitude before opening the door and entering the house. Sheena was on the phone in the kitchen and motioned for Lyric to come where she was. Most of the time Sheena had a house full of people, card games going on, top of the line designer knock off bag parties, you name it and it went down at her house. It was the local hangout.

Walking past the living room, Lyric noticed Kendra and another girl playing the Wii and lounging all over the contemporary beige leather sofa Lyric had just purchased for Sheena a few months ago on one of her generous home makeover shopping sprees. A sofa that was now ripped in several places along with numerous cigarette burns.

To see how badly Sheena had taken care of the furniture showed Lyric just how much she really appreciated her gift. *Fuck being generous with this girl,* Lyric thought.

Kendra paused the game when she saw Lyric walk past. "What up cuz?"

Lyric spoke by just throwing up her hand with a slight wave after she shot Kendra a "What the fuck are you doing here" stare and then walked into the kitchen, while waiting for Sheena to get off the phone. Lyric gave a quick surveillance of the house. The place was a complete mess. The first thing she noticed was all the dirty dishes piled up in the sink and a huge cob web in one of the corners. The floors looked like they hadn't been swept in months.

"How can she live like this," Lyric softly said to herself, as she continued looking around noticing the trashcan overflowing. "This is some nasty shit."

At that moment, Sheena ended her phone call. "Lyric, haven't you seen me calling you?"

"Yeah, I saw it…and," Lyric nonchalantly responded.

"I was calling to tell you that your cousin was staying here for a few months."

"Why? Wasn't that episode at the hotel enough for you or do you like that type of shit?" Lyric wondered why Diva hadn't mentioned anything about Kendra being there.

Sheena smiled. "Girl, it's not what you think. We just hanging out and having fun. Nothing serious."

Lyric just looked at Sheena and shook her head. She knew Kendra was probably listening to them and decided to wait until she had Sheena alone to talk to her. "And who is that other girl?"

"Her name is Pam. She's Kendra's friend, I guess."

"What do you mean, you guess?" Lyric inquired. "And she looks like somebody beat her ass, so you need to know."

Changing the subject, Sheena asked, "So, Lyric how you

and Diva end up together? I saw her ass come in here grinning with all those bags. I don't know why you wasting your time. Diva's ass ain't trying to do nothing but run around with old-ass men. Don't let her ass fool you." When Lyric didn't reply, Sheena continued. "I'm tired of trying to talk to her ass, she thinks she knows every fucking thing, but I told her if she gets pregnant, her ass is up out of my house." Sheena began to yell. "Diva get in here and clean this kitchen up!"

Seconds later, Diva came in the kitchen smacking her lips." Sheena, you tripping, I cleaned it up this morning and those damn dikes dirtied it up again. Why are they here anyway? They got the whole house smelling like weed!" Diva shouted toward the living room.

Kendra instantly stopped playing the game. "Yo, Sheena, control your daughter before I slap the shit out of her. I'm tired of her fuckin' mouth."

"Watch your mouth, girl," Sheena said shaking her head.

Lyric didn't say a word as she listened to her cousin who she barely knew anymore. She wasn't the kind, humble person she used to know.

"Sheena, come ride with me for a minute," Lyric suggested. "I have to go take care of my phone bill," she lied. Lyric really just wanted to get Sheena out of the house so she could talk to her in private.

"Alright, as long as you take me by the liquor store on the way back. I need some cigarettes and I'm sure Kendra will want a beer." Sheena walked toward her bedroom to get her purse wearing a pair of leggings and a short Christian Audigier t-shirt.

As Lyric stood waiting, she saw Kendra get up and follow Sheena into the bedroom. "Where the fuck you think you going?" Kendra asked with an attitude.

"To the store. Damn, can I breathe?" Sheena shot back.

Instantly, Kendra took her hand and slapped Sheena so hard, she fell back onto the dresser. "Sheena, don't make me go the fuck off in here. I don't care if you are going with my cousin

146

or not. Don't ever disrespect me like that. You got it?" When Sheena gave a weak head nod, Kendra kept going. "Cover your ass up with that little t-shirt on. Your ass giggling every where, and that shit is unacceptable."

A few minutes later, Sheena came out the room with a much longer shirt on and a pair of sunglasses. The slap already had her face red.

"Later cuz," Kendra said, as they two women walked out the house.

Lyric responded with a head nod. As soon as they got inside and Lyric cranked the car, she started going off. "Sheena, why did you let Kendra talk to Diva like that?"

Sheena sighed. "Please Lyric, don't start. Diva is a big girl. She can take care of herself."

"Do you think it's a good idea to have Kendra living with you? I mean, is her pussy eating skills that good?"

"Look, Kendra is my peoples. She just needed a spot to chill at for a few, since she got evicted."

"I can't believe you. She almost killed your ass at that hotel that night and you act like its okay. Next time I might not be around to save your ass. My cousin doesn't play games Sheena," Lyric warned. "I don't wanna see you in the same predicament as I'm in. I'm trying to get out a crazy relationship so you need to learn from me by not getting into one."

"She already apologized about that shit, okay? Damn, you starting to act just like Portia's booshie-ass. She's your damn cousin. You should be glad I'm helping her out."

"Okay, when the shit hits the fan, don't call me," Lyric said, turning the corner.

# Chapter 17

Lyric and Sheena pulled out of the liquor store parking lot thirty minutes later, but were halted by the sound of someone constantly beeping their horn. Lyric looked around to see where the noise was coming from then glanced in her rear view mirror to see Sasha's Lexus. It looked as if she was trying to get Lyric's attention as she flashed the lights and constantly blew the horn. Then suddenly, Sasha pulled in front of Lyric and blocked Diesel's car.

"Who the fuck is that?" Sheena asked with concern. She watched as Sasha jumped out the car like she was on a mission.

"That's Diesel's baby mama," "Lyric said, reaching in her purse. She wanted to get her razor just in case Sasha felt confident.

"What? Baby Mama? Oh, hell no!" Sheena yelled. She looked in her purse. "Shit, I forgot the box cutter Kendra gave me."

"You might need to use it on her if she keeps getting out of hand," Lyric replied.

"Diesel, please get out the car. I need to talk to you!" Sasha screamed at the top of her lungs while hitting the window. She was obviously unable to see through the dark tint.

When Lyric rolled down the window, Sasha reached her

head inside expecting to see Diesel. Her eyes widened when she didn't.

Sheena started yelling at that point. "Get the hell away from this car before I hurt your ass!"

"Lyric, I didn't know it was you," Sasha admitted. "But I'm glad it is. After I left your house the other day, Diesel called and threatened me. He started saying things like he was going to hurt me for coming over there and telling you about the twins. I need to talk to him and apologize. I need to make things right. I should've never come over there!"

"I can't believe you sitting here telling us this shit like we care. Bitch, didn't I tell you to get the hell away from this car," Sheena advised.

"Look, I don't know what you want me to do about it. I listened to you when you came to my damn house. I told you Diesel wasn't gonna take your threats lightly," Lyric stated.

"But you don't understand. He said he's gonna cut me off since I came to your house. I just want him to know that it was a mistake," Sasha continued to plead.

*Little do you know, what I have up my sleeve, he's not gonna have anymore money anyway*, Lyric thought to herself.

"But you're the reason he's mad at me, bitch. I don't even know why you were in the picture in the first place." Sasha's sweet demeanor had suddenly turned cold.

At that moment, Sheena jumped out the car, ran up on Sasha and punched her right in the face. Before Sasha could react, Sheena had managed to get two more punches in, making Sasha fall to the ground. It was if she had some built up frustration inside of her that desperately needed to come out.

"Oh, I got your bitch!" Lyric yelled out the window before slamming her foot on the gas pedal. After ramming into Sasha's car, she put the car in reverse then rammed the car again. Lyric did the same thing one last time before she'd moved Sasha's car out of the way.

After jumping back into the car, Sheena grabbed the forty ounce beer bottle she'd gotten for Kendra, rolled down the window and threw it in Sasha's direction at full speed. Luckily, the bottle only landed at her feet. "Don't let us catch you out in the street! Sheena yelled, as the car sped away. She looked at Lyric. "Why didn't you jump out and stomp that simple bitch?"

Lyric kept looking in the rear view mirror making sure they weren't being followed. "Fuck that. I refuse to fight over Diesel any longer."

"Well, I can," Sheena said with a smile. "Now, take me to another liquor store before Kendra beats my ass."

❤❤❤❤❤❤

Before taking Sheena back home, Lyric decided to treat her to a good meal at her favorite restaurant, The Crab Spot. While waiting for the first dozen crabs to arrive, they sat and discussed Diesel's baby mama then Sheena caught Lyric up on the latest gossip. Sheena knew everybody's business, who was at the club and who was trying to holla at who. Lyric listened as Sheena bragged about the shopping trip she was about to take to Atlanta with Kendra.

"Seriously, Sheena, you and Kendra really need to hold fast on this so called relationship," Lyric said. "That's my cousin and I love her, but she's just not right for you. Plus I know you're not completely giving up dick yet."

Sheena smiled then played with her hair. "I don't think I can give up dick like that either, but I guess I'm just confused. Kendra treats me better than any other nigga out here."

"What about money? You love that shit, and Kendra don't have paper like that. Who's financing this Atlanta trip? Who's paying for all the shopping? You're used to getting money from dudes not spending the shit on somebody else." Lyric knew Kendra would be pissed if she found out Lyric was being a hater on their so called relationship.

"Yeah, I can't stand that shit. I gotta pay for everything, and I don't roll like that. She do suck a mean clit though."

Lyric threw up her hand then looked down. "Shut up. I'm

not trying to hear that nasty shit!"

Just as Sheena was about to respond, Lyric looked back up and noticed Jabari walking through the restaurant with a take out bag. Lyric quickly called his name to get his attention, then waved him over.

"What up, Ma?" he asked. He had a thick New York accent like Diesel.

"Hey, Jabari," Lyric replied, giving him a fake friendly smile.

"Hey to you too, Jabari," Sheena said, batting her eyes. She always liked Jabari, but he never gave her the time of day.

"What up," he said, turning his attention back to Lyric. "Yo, let me holla at you for a second." Lyric got up and headed toward the front door with him. "Diesel has been tryin' to reach you. Answer yo' phone so the nigga will stop callin' me," Jabari informed.

Lyric frowned up her face then placed her hand on her hip. Lyric and Jabari were cool and Lyric often vented to him about Diesel. They would even talk sometimes for hours whenever Diesel was out of town or simply MIA. Although nothing sexual had ever taken place between the two of them, Jabari always came around at the right time which made Lyric feel connected to him. She often wondered how it would feel to be with him instead of Diesel.

"I'm sure you know what's going on right now, so I'll think about it," Lyric replied.

"Yeah, maybe we can talk 'bout that later." When Jabari glanced up at Lyric, he noticed the indescribable look in her eyes.

"You sure you aight?" Jabari asked, looking suspicious.

Lyric nodded her head indicating she was alright.

"If you need anythin', just holla, I got you," Jabari said.

"Thanks. I will." Lyric made sure she walked off with her ass sticking out. She knew Jabari would watch her walking away. He loved the way she walked; she had a Naomi Campbell walk for sure. The sight of her Coca Cola frame drove him crazy along with her ass cheeks which looked as if they were fighting for space in her tight jeans.

After dropping Sheena off an hour later, Lyric headed back home. She rode in complete silence thinking about her new life….away from Diesel and his drama. She decided to park in the driveway instead of the garage when she noticed a note stuck in the front door. She hopped out and grabbed the note and put the key in the door. Once inside, she read it.

## Get out of me and Diesel's life!!!

After reading the note, Lyric balled it up and threw it in the trash can then set the alarm. She knew the childish letter was from Sasha.

"Trust me, I'm trying, but I need to get some shit before I go," Lyric said.

Moments later, she went upstairs to her room cut on the lights, and to her surprise the room was filled with roses of all different colors. It was at least ten dozen.

"How the hell did those get in here?" Lyric began to wonder if Diesel had come back.

It was hard not to smile since she loved roses so much, but the smile soon turned into a frown when she read the note that was attached to one of the vases. She rolled her eyes before beginning to read.

Lyric baby, I'm sorry! I had planned to tell you about my daughters once I got back. Real talk. I don't care about Sasha. You know I love you and only you!!!! I hope you don't let this come between us. I'll be home Sunday morning, aight? I hope you like the roses, I had Jabari deliver them.

Lyric immediately tore up the note. "I'm leaving your ass, real talk that shit," she said mocking him. Lyric threw up the peace sign as if Diesel could see her.

Deciding to get ready for Vegas, Lyric walked over to her extra large walk in closet looking at all the clothes she had. It was filled to capacity and some clothes even still had tags on them. Furs, designer bags, tons of designer gear, it had all been bought with Diesel's money. Lyric knew it was time she became her own women. She was too dependant on Diesel.

She suddenly remembered her new jewelry and clothing that she'd gotten earlier then went downstairs and cut the alarm off. After going outside, Lyric popped the trunk of her car, then paused for a minute when she thought she heard a noise. She reached inside and grabbed the tire jack out the trunk, after looking around her quiet neighborhood.

"You getting ready to get fucked up if you keep playing with me, Sasha," Lyric said out loud. After not getting a response, Lyric soon realized that she was just being paranoid.

Gathering her new gear she closed the door, set the alarm and went back upstairs. While packing Lyric said to herself, "Diesel's ass is not gonna know what hit him."

# Chapter 18

Russell stood impatiently in the lobby waiting for Lyric to arrive. After some heavy convincing, she'd finally agreed to come to his hotel and park her car. Lyric didn't quite understand why she just wasn't meeting him at the airport, but little did she know, Russell had rented a limo so they could ride to the airport in style. He hadn't even had the money from the Remo job for twenty-four hours and he was splurging already.

His heart began to beat fast at the thought of finally spending time with Lyric all alone. Even if she was under the impression they were going as friends, Russell knew if he got her away, he would win her over. When his new pre-paid phone started vibrating, Russell hoped it wasn't Lyric calling to say that she'd changed her mind and wasn't coming.

"Damn, I don't want any bad news. Maybe I shouldn't have called her from this number earlier," he said, pulling the phone out of his pocket. However, Russell was relieved when he realized it was Ski; another person he'd called from his new toy. "I'll call his ass back later," Russell stated before putting the phone back.

Deciding to kill some anxious time, Russell made his way to the bathroom near the lobby. He checked his image in the mirror for the fifth time that day eyeing the new Hugo Boss button down shirt and three-hundred dollar Theory jeans he'd bought at the mall early that morning. There was no way Russell was about to board a plane with Lyric looking like a bum. After rubbing a few wrinkles out his shirt, Russell made his way back toward the front door. Suddenly, a wide smile appeared on his face as he watched Lyric finally pull up in her white Range Rover. She looked stunning in a pair of white Christian Dior sun glasses with DIOR in big letters on the side. He knew her shit was official, too. Lyric never wore knock off anything.

When she stepped out the truck, her tight skinny-leg jeans suffocated her fat ass. The matching cream colored Bebe top hung loosely off her right shoulder exposing the tattoo that read, *Mama Moses;* a tattoo that she, Portia and Russell all had in different areas. Her cute ankle strap Giuseppe sandals showed off her perfectly French manicured toes. Standing with her hands on her hips, she looked over at the valet, and pointed in the direction of her bags. Russell walked over and hugged her.

"Yo, you ready for some fun in Vegas?" Russell asked.

"Yes, I need to get away from this place and clear my head," Lyric answered then looked around. "What are you doing at the Westin? I thought you were staying at the Holiday Inn?"

"I was. I'll tell you about it later, for now let's bounce," Russell said, opening the door of the limo for Lyric to get inside.

"What the hell?" Lyric asked stepping inside. She wondered how Russell could afford a limo and a new hotel.

As soon as the driver pulled off and Russell instructed the driver where to go, Lyric peeped Russell's expensive watch and new wardrobe.

"Oh, shit. I see traits of the old Russell coming back. He definitely has stepped his game up, that's for sure. I know he hit somebody up. That watch looks almost like the one Diesel has, and I know how much that shit costs. Damn, I hope Russell doesn't go over the top like he did back in the day," Lyric said to herself.

"You straight, Lyric? Do you need anything before the

flight?" Russell asked.

"What you been up to, Russ? Where did you get the money for this limo? Plus, I see you been shopping," Lyric stated. She couldn't hide her curiosity.

"You don't need to worry about all that. Just know I'll take care of all the expenses on this trip now. Besides, don't you like men with money? That's why you in the predicament you in to start with."

Lyric rolled her eyes at Russell but didn't even bother to argue back. *Shit he is right*, she thought.

When they arrived at the airport a few minutes later, Lyric got out of the limo and walked up to the Jet Blue sky cap to check in her three bags. Russell however decided to carry his small bag on the flight. He'd packed extremely light with plans of shopping for more once he hit Sin City.

Just as Lyric was about to hand the sky cap her ID, her phone rang. It was Diesel… again. He'd been calling her non-stop since she arrived home and saw all the flowers. Lyric knew at this point, she had to talk to him or he would call continuously throughout her trip.

"Yeah," she answered in a dry nonchalant tone.

"Damn, it's about time you answer yo' fuckin' phone," Diesel said. By his harsh tone, Lyric could tell that he was pissed.

"What is it Diesel?"

"What is it? This is yo' damn man callin'. You better fix yo' tone, Ma. Now look, you've had enough time to mourn over that shit from the other day."

"That shit? You mean that shit about you having twin daughters? So, I'm just supposed to get over it like it's that easy?"

"Listen Lyric, real talk. I'd planned to tell you, but I knew yo' ass couldn't handle it and would react just like you actin' right now."

"Whatever, Diesel!"

"Whatever? Lyric don't make me have to straighten yo'

ass out when I get home. You know I love you. This shit is nothin'. Brush that shit off just like all the other shit that tries to come between us. We thicker than thieves', right?"

Lyric knew arguing with him wouldn't get her where she needed to be. Right now she needed to be his ride or die type chick. "You're right, baby. Nothing can come between us," Lyric agreed. She wanted to vomit as soon as those words came out of her mouth.

"That's more like it. I'll see you tomorrow. Make sure you have yo' ass at home, too because we need to talk."

Lyric frowned. "Tomorrow?"

Her tone instantly made Diesel upset and somewhat suspicious. "Yeah, tomorrow. Why? Is there somethin' you need to tell me?"

"No, I just thought you were coming home Sunday morning."

"Well, I changed my mind."

Russell watched Lyric as she stood in line on her phone. He could tell she was having a heated conversation. "It's probably with that nigga, Diesel. I hate that she keeps letting him put her through so much bullshit," he said to himself.

Lyric hung up and felt like tossing her phone into the street.

Russell saw Lyric walking in his direction with a puzzled expression.

"Is everything alright," he asked.

"I'm sorry Russ, but I can't go to Vegas. Diesel is coming home early."

"So, what does that have to do with us?"

"No, you don't understand. I can't just be gone like that, and he not know where I am. But you should still go and enjoy yourself."

"Naw, fuck that. I wanted us to go together. Why is that nigga coming back so soon anyway?"

Lyric asked the sky cap not to place a baggage claim tag on her luggage, grabbed her bag, then walked away without an-

swering Russell's question. She didn't feel like talking about
Diesel at the moment. The limo driver had already left so Lyric
flagged down a cab. After putting their luggage in the trunk,
they both jumped in and headed back to Russell's hotel. He was
silent during the ride and looked out the window. He was pissed
at Diesel for ruining his time alone with Lyric. His eyes were
red with a crazy demonic look in them.

*Damn, there goes my getaway to Vegas, shit,* Lyric
thought.

When the cab pulled up to Russell's hotel a few minutes
later, he got out with an attitude. He couldn't believe Lyric had
changed her mind.

"Russell, can I come up? I need to talk to you about
something," Lyric stated.

Russell finally pepped up. "Of course." Russell grabbed
her bags out of the back seat then headed to his room, which had
been upgraded to a suite, of course.

Once inside, Russell adjusted the air condition. He'd left
it on by mistake, so the room was freezing. He grabbed a blan-
ket off the bed and covered Lyric as she sat on the couch.

"Thanks Russ, I know you're upset with me right now,
but once I fill you in, you'll understand."

"Understand what?" Russell was starting to get a
headache and hoped it wasn't another episode coming on. He
grabbed his head. *Maybe I need to go get that prescription
filled, so I can control myself.*

"Are you okay?"

"Yeah, I'm fine. Go ahead."

"Russ, I need you to help me rob Diesel."

Russell was completely caught off guard. "What?"

"I'm serious. He has a large amount of money at his
stash house." Lyric had already ransacked their home and
checked both of his safes in an attempt to find large sums of
cash, but came up empty

"How do you know? It could be somewhere else."

"Trust me. It has to be there. I know for a fact, he doesn't keep it in our house. I've looked on multiple occasions. I mean he has a small stash at home, which I raid all the time, but I need the real money. I've been putting up with his bullshit too long not to walk away with something." Lyric looked at Russell. "Will you help me?" She then moved over closer to him and sealed the deal with a soft kiss on his lips. "I'll definitely give you a portion of the money."

Russell was in complete heaven after feeling her soft lips. He paused for a minute before responding. "How much we talking?"

"At least twenty percent."

"Damn right, I'm down. This is my type of shit anyway, but it's different with Diesel. You love the nigga, so I hope you're really serious about this. I need you to swear to secrecy." *I would hate to hurt Lyric, but I will if she crosses me, snitches or shit even if she stays with the nigga. I have no plans on going back to prison,* Russell thought.

"I swear Russell, you have my word. I'm done with his ass after this."

"Are you sure you searched your crib real good?" Russell asked, scratching his chin.

"Trust me, I've searched that place like I work for the damn Feds."

"Humm, let me see. Who works for him? How many niggas on his team?"

"Just one. Diesel doesn't trust anybody, so he only deals with his friend, Jabari. They grew up together and are like brothers. He even moved from New York to Charlotte for him."

"Does he like you?"

Lyric hesitated. "Yeah…I guess."

Russell shook his head. "Good, then you need to go after his ass tonight. He's gonna be the one who gives up the information about the stash house. You may even have to have sex with him in order to get it, but just make sure you wear a condom."

Lyric scrunched up her eyebrows. "Are you serious?"

"Yeah, I am. You gotta get him comfortable enough to

tell you something and nothing will do that better than pussy." He hated telling Lyric to have sex with anyone else other than him, but it had to be done. "Once you're done, come back and fill me in as soon as you get the info. Here, you can even take my room key in case I'm not here when you get back."

Lyric grabbed the key card and placed it in her purse and took out her phone and called Jabari. After hearing her on the phone, Russell went straight to the bathroom to calm himself down when thoughts about Lyric possibly having sex with someone else crossed his mind. He then thought about his wife and her betrayal. "Yeah, I fucked another man," the voices began to say. "You couldn't satisfy me, Russell!"

After pacing the floor, he punched the glass mirror, causing a large chunk to fall into the sink. Needing to feel some pain, Russell took the glass and dug it into the palm of his hand until blood began to drip onto the floor. He began to grit his teeth.

"I'm only doing this so we can be together," he said in a low tone. "We have to be together."

# Chapter 19

Lyric turned into the Mint Worth Village subdivision and approached the address Jabari had given her. After finally reaching the house, she tilted her head to the side.

"Damn this house is nice, I wonder who lives here," Lyric asked herself.

She put the truck in park and immediately started primping herself in one of her small compact mirrors. After touching up her lip-gloss and hair, Lyric got out and glanced at her clothes. "Perfect," she said to herself.

After leaving Russell, she'd gone back home took a long hot shower and rubbed her body down with her favorite Japanese Blossom lotion just in case she had to rock Jabari's world. She had to look extra sexy in order for her plan to be successful.

However, the more she thought about what she was doing, the more pissed off Lyric was about what she had to do in order to get any information. It pissed her off that Diesel didn't trust her enough to tell where his money was, but she knew he had trust issues and he felt that all the dirt he did to people would one day come back to haunt him. And he was right...Karma was a bitch and in this case her name was Lyric.

Jabari watched Lyric walk up from the window with her

shades on looking all Hollywood, even though it was night time. He was mesmerized by her beauty. Jabari had wanted Lyric ever since the first night he laid eyes on her at the CIAA event. He recalled trying to make his way over to meet her that night, but Diesel rushed past him and got to her first. They were always in competition. He never wanted Jabari to out do him and Lyric was the baddest thing in the club that night, so it wasn't even up for discussion who was going to get her.

He remembered when he first hugged her after consoling her over something Diesel had done. He was hypnotized when he felt her soft skin. She felt like silk, smooth and soft. He fantasized about how it would feel to make love to her all night.

Lyric rang the door bell breaking his chain of thoughts. Jabari opened the door looking her up and down noticing how good she looked in her sexy black Dolce & Gabbana strapless dress that showed all of her cleavage.

"What's up P.Y.T.?" Jabari always called her that, which meant Pretty Young Thing, when Diesel wasn't around, and as corny as it sounded, Lyric loved it. "Come on in, me casa is your casa."

"This is your house, Jabari?" Lyric asked surprised.

She stood doing a double take with a particular look on her face. Surprised that this was his home and it looked like something out of a magazine. It was absolutely gorgeous. "Diesel never mentioned to me that Jabari was living like this. From the looks of things, he is doing the damn thing," she said casing the joint out. Lyric sat down on the couch pulling off her shoes, she didn't want to get his off-white carpet dirty.

"Yeah, it's mine."

Lyric wondered to herself why she always assumed the run down house on Freedom Street was his.

Looking at Lyrics toes freshly done almost made Jabari lose his mind. He also noticed the sad look on her face.

"What's wrong?" he asked, rubbing her face softly with the outside of his hand.

Lyric immediately broke down putting her actress skills

to work, blinking her eyes until she was able to build up some tears. "It's over between me and Diesel. I'm tired of him." She paused for a moment. "Truth be told, I can't hide my feelings for you anymore."

Jabari's eyes widened. "Your feelings for me?"

"Yeah, for you. Why do you think I always run to you when he fucks up? I love the attention and strong arms you always give me."

"Damn, I' on know, Diesel is fam. I don't want to get in the middle of this," Jabari said, walking over taking a seat on the edge of the couch.

Lyric could see the hesitation on his face, but could also see the lust in his green eyes. "Fuck Diesel. He doesn't give a damn about you. All he does is shit on you, saying, "Jabari aint shit, Jabari wanna be me. He is so jealous of you."

Jabari seemed surprised. "Word."

"Yeah. I told him once that he needed to be more like you and he flipped out. He grabbed me by the neck and told me if I ever compared him to you or mentioned your name he would kill my ass."

Jabari shook his head. "Damn, Ma. Sorry you had to go through that."

"I hate to get you mixed up in all of this, but I can't help the way I feel, the way I've always felt." Lyric stood up and took off her clothes and sat back down on the couch butt naked with her legs crossed. "So, you telling me, you don't' want this?" She then uncrossed her legs so he could see her pretty pink pussy.

Jabari stared at Lyric, for the first time in his life not knowing what to do. It felt as if his heart was about to come out of his chest. She was so beautiful and her body was even better than he'd ever imagined it to be.

At that moment, Lyric could sense his nervousness and decided to make the first move; she was sick of playing with him. "Jabari, I want you and I need you," she said rubbing her hands across her breast.

The adrenaline rushed through his body. He couldn't take it anymore. "Get your ass over here!" he said, pulling her close to him. He kissed her right in the mouth.

"Damn," she moaned while pushing him back and sliding off his shirt.

He placed his hands on her shapely thighs and instantly felt his dick getting hard as he slowly rubbed his hands up and down her legs. Lyric then pulled him to his feet as she dropped down and removed his white air force ones. Jabari didn't waste anytime un- buttoning his belt and loosening his Citizens of Humanity jeans, causing them to fall to the floor.

Moments later, he stepped out of his jeans still admiring Lyrics naked body in front of him. Suddenly, she moved in close to him pulling his boxers to his ankles then sucking his dick in her forceful way. She was known in her days to always turn a nigga out.

He moaned and groaned like he was a virgin getting head for the very first time.

After a very large orgasm, Jabari flipped Lyric over on the couch with her legs spread like an eagle. Without hesitating. he dove in sucking and licking on her pussy while his tongue did circular motions around her clit-driving Lyric crazy. She moaned louder when she felt his warm mouth touch her insides. He continued by licking her perky breast along with her large and protruding nipples, which drove Jabari mad.

Lyric kissed him seductively as he handled her breasts with extreme care. She was ready for everything he had to give. Lyric pulled out a condom and gently slid it onto his ten inch dick. She then tilted her head back in pleasure as he entered her, moving in and out using deep, passionate thrusts. She moved her hips and threw the pussy back to him.

"Oh, shit right there," Lyric moaned. She hadn't felt a dick this good inside of her in a long time...not even Diesel's. *Hell, his dick was more like an eight inch anyway.*

He pumped in and out of her pussy so hard; she felt herself cumming and grabbed him by the neck. His stamina was out of this world as they made love non-stop for hours until their bodies laid weak and lifeless.

After lying in each others sweaty arms for a while trying to catch their breath, Lyric turned to Jabari pulling him close letting him know her true feelings once again. "You know, Diesel is going to flip when he finds out I'm leavin' him for you. But, we haven't been happy for the past two years. He spends more time with his other bitches than he does at home with me, and I'm tired of it."

"Yeah, Diesel is off the hook wit' that shit. I tried to tell him that you were a good girl, but the nigga don't listen."

Lyric smiled. "Well, he should've taken your advice. I mean come on Jabari, he had twin daughters that I didn't even know anything about."

All Jabari could go was shake his head.

"Did you ever help him out? Like at that old-ass house on Freedom Street where I actually thought you lived. Did he ever take any of his women there?" Lyric questioned. She hoped this bait would lead to other important information.

"No, that's his stash spot. He would never take women there."

Lyric almost choked even though she hadn't drank anything. "Are you serious? That's the stash house?" Lyric was completely floored. The run-down house that she'd been to on several occasions was actually the stash house.

Russell's plan worked. Jabari had sung like a canary telling her exactly what she'd come for. She was kind of upset that she'd given him some pussy for nothing even though it was a good nut.

"Lyric, you can lay low over here for awhile to get yourself together and decide how to deal wit' Diesel. He doesn't know 'bout this spot out here. I just moved in," Jabari said, breaking her train of thought.

"So, do you care if he finds out about us?" she questioned.

"No, not at all. I've been meaning to get a new employer

for a while now anyway. Diesel's even been shady wit' me lately."

    She was thrown back after hearing how Jabari really felt. He was willing to cross Diesel and give up the long time friendship they shared just to be with her. It was nice to be wanted again, but she didn't have time for broken promises anymore. She shook it off remembering her reason for being there. Her plan…the heist.

    Now all she had to do was go report back to Russell with the info. He would stake the joint out so they could break in and steal the money and Lyric could leave town disappearing on all of their asses.

# Chapter 20

Diva looked in the mirror holding up a blue BCBG jersey mini dress. "Nawww, this won't work either," she said, tossing another outfit down in frustration.

"Damn, none of these clothes look right. I got to be hot tonight for my date with King."

She sat down on her bed that was covered with clothes she attempted to wear. Even though she'd just gone shopping with Lyric, nothing seemed to be good enough for the occasion. Suddenly she thought of her mother's new Miu Miu designer dress that she hadn't even worn yet.

"Oh, hell yeah, that would be perfect to rock tonight. Sheena is gonna flip if she finds out cause her selfish-ass never likes to share her shit, but she'll be alright. If it wasn't that, she would find something to bitch at me about anyway," Diva said, headed to her mother's room.

Since Sheena was in Atlanta for a few days, Diva prayed she hadn't carried the dress with her. She did the stanky leg dance when she saw the dress hanging in Sheena's closet still wrapped in plastic with the tags attached. She carried the red empire waist dress back to her room and slowly removed the plastic making sure not to mess it up so she could put it back.

After admiring the dress that screamed vixen, Diva slid it on, tucked the tag inside and smiled in the mirror at the outcome.

"This dress is so hot, but not as hot as the bitch wearing it," she said, touching up her makeup and combing down her Doobie wrap. Her long hair fell on her shoulders as she shook it one last time.

Suddenly she heard her Nikki Minaj ringtone going off on her cell phone indicating she had a text message. When she viewed the text it was Russell saying that he was outside. She slipped on a pair of Gucci sandals that had the famous red and green strap going across foot and grabbed her new Bvlgari purse before running out the door.

Upon her entering Russell's car, he watched as Diva walked over like a professional model. "I'm glad I came out. I needed to get out in order to get Lyric sleeping with that nigga Jabari off my mind. I've been calling and she hasn't answered her phone. Maybe this little freak can help me pass the time," he told himself.

"Hey King, I'm glad you finally called," she said once she sat down in the front seat.

"What's up, boo?" he responded looking at her curves in the sexy dress she was wearing. His dick began to get hard just thinking about her pussy.

Russell pulled off and turned up his Usher CD, as the slow song, *Papers* flowed through the speakers. Diva looked over at Russell seductively; he returned the look licking his tongue across his lips. She was feeling him and wanted him to know just how much. After riding for awhile, the mood was set, so she reached over as he was driving and unzipped his jeans.

"That's what's up," he said, realizing what Diva was about to do.

She pulled his dick out, slid her head down in his crotch then opened her mouth nice and wide. At first, Diva gagged not realizing it was so huge, but quickly adjusted his manhood in her mouth determined to give him the best head he'd ever had in his life. After finding her groove, she sucked, licked, stroked and pulled on it hoping Russell didn't have a wreck after hearing his loud moans.

He looked down at Diva; something about her was so familiar. "Damn bitch, you suck a mean dick." He decided to pull over in the nearest parking lot so he could concentrate on the good, sloppy head she was putting down.

After putting the car in park, he pulled her beautiful hair back so he could see her in motion. Seconds later, his phone vibrated which instantly pissed him off. After looking at it and ignoring a call from Lyric, his head rolled back in the seat as Diva sucked with force giving him more than enough pleasure. He pushed her head down, pumping his dick in her mouth. When he couldn't take it any longer he told her to stop, he had to get some of that pussy.

"Come here," Russell said, putting his seat all the way back.

Diva climbed on top of him in the driver's seat and he put his dick inside her.

"Wait…aren't you going to use a condom?" Diva asked, scared she might get pregnant or catch a disease. The last thing she needed was to get pregnant and have to hear Sheena's mouth.

Russell ignored her and forcefully fucked her hard. Diva tried to ease up some so it wouldn't hurt so bad. Russell was huge and she couldn't handle it. She was use to dick, but not that big. He grabbed onto her back and pulled her close hitting her pussy with hard, deep thrusts. She held onto the back of the seat and started grinding him back.

"That's what the fuck I'm talking about, give me that pussy bitch!" Russell said.

A few minutes later Diva felt Russell's body shaking and he let out a loud grunt as he reached an orgasm and took his dick out and released his nut all over her face.

*This bitch is definitely a keeper, she got skills,* Russell thought. *Even if Lyric do become my girl, I still gotta keep this broad around.* The entire scene that just took place reminded him of the movie, *Belly* when the young cutie was giving DMX head in the car and his girl called. *This bitch is doing a good job taking my mind off Lyric for the moment.*

Once Diva was finished, she wiped her mouth and stared at Russell waiting to see his reaction. When he didn't say anything, she decided to ask him herself. "So, was I any good?"

Russell smiled. "Damn, right. I ain't had a head job like that in a minute. As a matter of fact, it's been years. I used to know this girl back in the day, who could put in work like that." Diva had no idea that he was talking about her own mother.

"Well, you got me now, so it's no need to think about that bitch anymore."

Russell stared at Diva's skin, which looked as if she suffered from acne. "I meant to ask this before, how old are you?"

She lied and told Russell she was a twenty-seven year old nurse and a college graduate from UNC. Even though, he could care less how old she was. Someone giving head like that had to have some age on them. On the way to Aquavina Steak and Seafood Restaurant, Russell actually found himself enjoying their date so far. The conversation with Diva was fun and lively, which surprised him. She had a sense of humor and kept Russell laughing. She was also interesting, sweet, smart and beautiful.

Right before they turned on Tyron Street, Russell saw Lyric's number come up on his phone again. This time, he decided to answer. "What's up?"

"Hey, Russ, are you busy?"

"Naw, not really," he replied. She didn't need to know about Diva. "You get the info?"

"Yes, I did. I'll meet you back at your hotel in about thirty minutes."

"Actually, I may need a little longer than that, but you have the key just in case you get there before me, right?"

"Yes, I have it. I'll see you then." Lyric replied before hanging up.

Russell stopped the car in the middle of the street and did

a quick u-turn before heading back the way that'd just came.

"What's going on? You were going in the right direction," Diva stated.

"Change of plans. Something came up. I gotta drop you back off at home."

"But I thought we were going to chill together tonight." Diva said pissed and irritated. "After I just sucked your dick, you gonna play me like that. What's up?"

"Bitch, don't question me. I got business to handle. I'll come pick you up tomorrow and maybe take you shopping if you act right."

All the fun and laughing during the date and was over now. Money was on the line. He had to get that paper.

"This is some bullshit."

Not wanting to hear her mouth anymore, Russell reached into his pocket and pulled out ten one hundred dollar bills. "That should be more than enough to shut your ass up for now."

And it was. After grabbing the money, Diva sat back in her seat, thinking about the new Juicy watch she wanted along with a few other things. In her mind, Russell was definitely about to be her new sugar daddy.

# LOVE HEIST

# Chapter 21

Lyric pulled into Russell's hotel parking lot and got out of the truck. She hoped Russell was in his room because she wanted to tell him the info about Diesel's stash spot and head home. She actually didn't want to go upstairs, but decided to anyway. The last thing she needed was for Russell to get mad at her and decide not to help her out. Lyric needed to soak in the tub to make sure her pussy was good and tight when Diesel got home. He often accused her of cheating when he came home from a trip saying her pussy felt loose. She could only imagine what he would feel fucking behind Jabari's big dick.

As she headed into the hotel, she had no idea that Russell was inside pacing the floor back and forth. Almost an hour had passed since Lyric called telling him she had information about Diesel's stash spot. All kinds of crazy thoughts were going through his mind. He wondered what she had to do to get the information and how many times she'd done it.

"I hate to have to kill that nigga. That's my pussy!" Russell yelled. "What the fuck is taking her so long? I could'a got that bitch Diva to suck me off one more time if I'd known Lyric was gonna take all fucking day. She better hurry up."

He paced back and forth, trying to think of something other than Lyric fucking Jabari when he finally heard a knock at the door. Russell didn't even bother to look out the peep hole, but just yanked it open.

"Damn, it took you a long time to get over here. You must think a nigga don't have shit else to do other than sit here waiting for your ass."

Lyric didn't care for his tone. "Sorry, Russ. Since I never got anything to eat, I was hungry so I went by the Waffle House first. You said to give you a minute anyway, so I wasn't rushing." She stood and waited for him to reply, wondering why he was acting so strange. She then turned to lighten the mood when she realized he smelled like a woman's perfume.

"Where the hell you been?" Lyric said, with a smirk on her face. "You smell like a woman."

"And you smell like you been fucking. Have you?" Russell asked.

Lyric wondered where his attitude was coming from. She tried to ignore his question. "Look, this is some crazy shit. I found out that I knew where his stash spot was the entire time. It's an old house on Freedom Street. I've been over there with Diesel several times thinking it was Jabari's crib, because that's what Diesel always told me, but it wasn't. I never went inside, though." She looked at Russell, who was staring back at her like a mad man. "So, what's next? You stake it out and then what? How are we going to get in to search the joint without a key?"

"You let me worry about all that. I got this, just like we did it back in the day. You and Portia got me the address and I took care of the rest. All you need to do is wait for the money." Russell scratched his face. "Did you fuck him, Lyric?"

Lyric knew she had to answer him because he wasn't trying to let up. "How else was I going to get the address, Russell?" She sat down on the couch.

Russell walked over and sat down beside her. He then leaned in and tried to give Lyric a kiss.

"What the hell you doing?" Lyric asked.

"I just want a kiss. Is that wrong?" All of a sudden, Russell began to hear voices. *That bitch is trying to hold out.*

Lyric didn't want to piss Russell off, but she also didn't want to lead him on, especially not now. She'd already just fucked one guy for some information she knew all along, so she didn't want to fuck Russell just for his help as well. Lyric had to think of another approach. "No, Russ it's not wrong. It's just that, things are moving so fast right now. I think I just wanna get things over with Diesel first, before moving on with someone else."

Russell's nostrils began to flare. "Shit, you gave that nigga Jabari the pussy, now I can't even get a kiss?" *Slap that bitch for trying to play you*, the voices said.

"Russ please, it's not like that. Besides, you're the one who told me to sleep with him. Why are you acting like this?"

*Man, that's your pussy. I told you to take that shit before*, the voices continued. All of a sudden Russell stood up, then slapped Lyric across the face.

Lyric grabbed her stinging face in complete shock. "What the hell is wrong with you?" she said, getting up. Lyric tried to move toward the door when Russell grabbed her by the hair and pushed her down on the bed. After slapping her again, he forcefully held her down, then began to rip off her dress. "Get off of me!" Lyric screamed.

However, Russell ignored her demands. Instead, he punched her in the face and forced her to turn over on her stomach while he tied up her hands and legs with a sheet that he tore in half. When he finished, he reached in the drawer beside the bed and pulled out a pair of his socks then stuffed them in her mouth. Russell wished he had some duck tape. Going another route, he took a thinner dress sock and managed to tie it around her mouth to hold the silencer in place. "You know all this could've been avoided if you would've just gave me the pussy years ago instead of walking around teasing me."

After that he tore her panties off then stared at her smooth, round ass. He could also see parts of her manicured vagina, which made his manhood thump. Once it was nice and hard, Russell rammed his huge dick inside her from behind, fucking Lyric hard and deep.

Lyric instantly tried to get loose but the sheets were just too tight. She moaned and begged for him to stop even though he couldn't hear her. She listened as he spoke in the voice of a true maniac.

Russell began to yell obscenities as he banged her head against the headboard. "All y'all are just alike. My mother, my wife and now you. None of y'all bitches ever loved me. All of y'all just want to leave. I thought you were special!"

After a few more long and deep strokes, Russell was really into it. He drove his dick deep inside her pussy like he wanted to find her fallopian tubes. Lyric's body felt numb as Russell pounded away at her treasure like a jackhammer. The sounds of his balls slapping up against her ass sounded like an audience clapping at a concert.

"I knew this pussy was going to be good. I shoulda took it a long time ago," Russell admitted. He continued to thrust his dick in and out before his body began to jerk like he was having a seizure. A few seconds later, Russell yelled out, "Oh, shit...I'm cumming!"

As Lyric's body laid there helpless, Russell emptied loads of sperm inside of her then finally slowed down once his tool went limp. Little did Lyric know that was just the beginning. At that point, Russell turned her over, spread her legs, then made his way to her dripping pussy with his tongue. Under normal circumstances, Lyric probably would've enjoyed the feeling, but not this time. She continued to lay there like a corpse as tears made their way down her cheeks.

After about three hours of non stop fucking, Russell was finally finished. He'd even performed anal sex on Lyric, which really made her yell out in pain. It was the worst thing she'd ever experienced in life. After going into the bathroom to wash off all the sex, Russell walked back into the room to find Lyric fast asleep. Walking over to her, Russell began to rub his hands through her hair like they were a couple, then softly kissed her on the forehead.

"Sweet dreams, baby," he said, pulling the covers up on her naked body even though he still didn't untie her. "I'll be back to get some more of that good pussy in a few." He walked over to the couch to turn on the T.V. when he heard Lyric's phone vibrating in her purse. At first, he was going to ignore it, but when it went off two more times, Russell got upset.

"It better not be that muthafucka Jabari or Diesel," he said, grabbing the phone. After moving the trackball to the messages icon, he softened a bit once he realized it was two text messages from Portia asking if Lyric could pick her and Charles up at the airport early the next morning. They were taking a red eye from Hawaii. Portia also said that they could've caught a cab, but just wanted to catch up on what she missed while they were gone.

Russell texted Portia back like it was Lyric and told her "okay". He then looked over at Lyric. "Portia is gonna be so happy when she finds out that we're finally together."

# LOVE HEIST

# Chapter 22

When Sheena and Kendra boarded their flight back to Charlotte, Sheena took a seat exhausted from the short two day trip in the ATL. She quickly realized it was a mistake when shortly after arriving, Kendra started to express her feelings about being in love and wanting to spend the rest of her life with Sheena. However, what Kendra didn't know was that Sheena wasn't trying to be with a woman for the rest of her life. She was just confused and really preferred a man beside her at night anyway. She'd just been hurt by so many men in her life that she didn't know which way to turn. She didn't trust men anymore, especially since her father molested her from the age of eleven to seventeen. Then she started messing with Russell a year later, who she fell in love with, but he ended up beating her and left her for dead.

Sheena didn't want to spoil the trip so she decided to break things off with Kendra once they got home. Not to mention, she needed to call Lyric for back up because she knew Kendra was crazy.

Sheena fastened her seat belt when she heard the pilot come over the loud speaker. She glared out the window thinking about Diva. She needed to come clean and tell her about Russell being her father. She always imagined once Diva got a

certain age she would come to her and ask about her father but
she never had.

"How do you tell your daughter her father never wanted
her and beat the shit of me trying to make sure she was never
born? But she survived," Sheena said to herself.

She hadn't even told Lyric and Portia the truth. However,
after all these years of carrying around the guilt baggage, it was
time for her to come clean regardless of who it might hurt. Her
fucked up childhood and devastating episode with Russell had
her bitter. Sheena had the "I don't give a fuck attitude," but it
was starting to get old and take its toll on her. She felt herself
wiping away tears as she reflected back on her wild and crazy
lifestyle. Stripping, tricking and being a horrible mother.

Sheena felt bad about the way she had treated her own
daughter. *Diva never asked to be bought into this world*, Sheena
thought. Even after the neglect Diva endured, she still was
smart, strong and beautiful. Sheena loved her daughter, but
often blamed her for the pain Russell caused. Russell had really
fucked Sheena's head up and getting revenge on him was something she longed for instead of focusing on Diva.

Sheena was going to work on her relationship with her
daughter if it wasn't too late. She even hoped that one day, Diva
could call her mom. Sheena reached in her new Valentino bag
that she'd just bought, grabbed a tissue and wiped away her
tears. *Hell, I might even confess to Lyric about what happened
between me and Diesel. I gotta get all this shit up off of me,*

"What the hell is wrong with you, Sheena?" Kendra
asked.

"Nothing, I just have some things on my mind."

"Well tell me about it, so I can try and help you. That's
what couples do."

Sheena looked at her sideways. "Couples, girl we aint no
damn couple! We need to talk once we get back to my house,"
Sheena said with an attitude.

Kendra bit her bottom lip then looked around the plane.
She felt herself getting angry, but decided to wait until they got

back to the house to beat Sheena's ass. She didn't want airport security on her ass once they landed. Not to mention, she was on her last month of parole, and didn't want to go back to prison, so she sat pissed off for the duration of the short one hour flight.

Once they finally landed, Sheena gathered her things, then turned on her cell phone to call Diva and make sure she was on her way to pick them up. Normally, she parked at the airport, but Diva bugged her for hours about letting her use the car while she was gone. Sheena guessed she wanted to put her new driver's license to the test.

She texted Diva letting her know that they'd landed. A few seconds later, Diva texted back that she and Pam were outside circling the terminal and to hurry up so airport security wouldn't be harassing them.

*What the hell is Pam doing with my daughter?* Sheena thought.

❤❤❤❤❤❤

As Pam circled the airport again, Diva thanked her for coming with her to pick up her mother. She'd tried calling Lyric to do it for her, but she never answered which was odd. "Sheena is going to flip out once she finds out that I wrecked her car," Diva said.

"She probably will. Kendra might, too," Pam replied.

Diva sucked her teeth. "I don't give a shit about Kendra. I'll be glad when my mother leaves her alone any damn way. Speaking of that, what's your relationship with Kendra anyway? Are y'all lovers, too? Is Sheena involved in a threesome?"

"We had some special moments, but that was back in the day. I only been around recently because I need her to do something for me," Pam replied.

When Diva was about to respond, she quickly told Pam to pull over once she saw Russell's rental car parked at Terminal A. She smiled to herself thinking about their night and the money he'd given her.

"Maybe if I can get away with sucking him off right here, he'll give me some more money," Diva said to herself. At that point, she wanted to text Sheena back to tell her to take her time.

Hopping out the car, Diva ran up to Russell's window then knocked. "Hey, King," she said, as he rolled it down. You couldn't wipe the smile off her face.

"What's up? What are you doing here? You following me?" Russell asked.

"No, I'm here to pick up my mother and her girl..." Diva paused. "And her friend."

"Really. That's what's up." When Russell thought he saw Charles coming out of the terminal, he got out the car and walked around to the trunk to help him and Portia with the bags, but it wasn't Charles.

"Well, since you out the car, give me a hug," Diva suggested.

Sheena walked out the double doors of Terminal B and immediately looked for Diva who wasn't outside. After wondering if she was circling the airport again, Sheena looked to the left then dropped her mouth when saw Diva several yards away at another terminal, hugging a guy. "I can't believe this shit. Here we are rushing to get outside, and she's all hugged up with some nigga."

Kendra looked in Diva's direction. "Yeah, you really raised a perfect young lady. She's filled with such class."

Sheena gave Kendra the look of death. *I can't wait to get rid of your ass.* As Sheena eyed the man who was now palming Diva's ass, she couldn't help but stare. He looked extremely familiar. She stared at the guy a few seconds longer, then suddenly her eyes widened. "Oh hell no, is that Russell?" Sheena said, dropping her Samsonite overnight bag. "Yeah, it is!" Sheena instantly took off running toward them. "Get your hands off her mutherfucker!" she began to shout. After reaching them, Sheena grabbed Diva and slung her away from Russell.

"Sheena, what's wrong with you? Why do you keep

doing this to me? Every guy I meet, you always start some shit!" Diva yelled.

"Diva this is not some guy. This bastard is your father!" Sheena fired back.

Russell's entire face dropped as he stared at Diva…his daughter. It wasn't until that very moment, when he realized how much she favored his late mother. Diva had her eyes, her hair, and her complexion. That's why she seemed so familiar to him.

"My father?" Diva questioned with concern.

"Yes, Russell is your father," Sheena replied. "Did you sleep with him?"

Diva quickly looked away, then back over at Russell and remembered the night she gave him head and fucked in his car and immediately started throwing up on the curb. At that same moment, Pam walked up and stared Russell down.

"You remember me?"

Russell looked at Pam, who he knew was the girl from the sports bar, but still wasn't fazed by her evil smirk. "Yeah, I do, so what?" It wasn't long before he started hearing voices in his head again. Without hesitation, Russell grabbed Sheena by the neck and started chocking her with both hands. "You bitch, you're a sorry-ass excuse for a mother. You're just like my mother. If you weren't out here fucking everything, you would be home taking care of our daughter. She shouldn't be out here fucking grown-ass men. I can't believe this!" He started tightening up his grip.

At that moment, Kendra starting running in Sheena's direction even though she was enjoying the fact that Sheena was getting her ass beat. She knew Sheena was about to put her out, so saving her wasn't her top priority. But she decided to go help the bitch anyway.

"This is the nigga I was telling you about!" Pam shouted as Kendra approached them. "Do something!"

Running up on Russell, Kendra swung on him, punching him several times in the face. She definitely had Laila Ali skills and even managed to get in a few kicks. Even though it looked as if none of the punches hurt, Russell quickly let Sheena go. As Sheena began gasping for air, Russell could see several other airport passengers pointing in their direction.

Russell pointed to Kendra. "Bitch consider yourself dead for that shit!"

Diva ran to her mother's side but kept a close watch on Russell at the same time.

At that moment, Russell ran and jumped back in his car and pulled off when he saw several men in security uniforms running in their direction. As he pulled off, both Portia and Charles walked out of the terminal looking extremely tanned and holding hands...newlywed style. Portia quickly dropped her husband's hand, when she saw Sheena sitting on the ground, with Diva rubbing her back, and Kendra standing over her. She immediately ran over toward them.

"What happened?" Portia asked.

"Russell attacked me," Sheena replied.

"That guy is fucking crazy!" Pam added.

"What? Are you serious?" Portia looked around. "Where's Lyric? Is she here? She was supposed to pick us up."

"I haven't seen Lyric," Kendra chimed in.

"What was Russell doing here?" Portia continued to drill.

"Maybe he was picking you up. I don't know," Diva said, as tears welled up in her eyes.

Portia wanted to ask more questions, but when security began to crowd around, Charles quickly pulled her away. "Let's go."

"But Charles, Sheena looks hurt."

"She'll be fine. You don't need to get involved in that mess, Portia. The next thing you know, I'll be on the 6:00 news. I have a reputation to uphold," Charles stated. "This is some straight Jerry Springer shit, and I don't want any parts of it. We'll just take a cab like I told you to do in the first place."

Portia was just about to debate with Charles, but then decided against it. In her mind, maybe he was right. Portia hadn't even been home an hour, and the same drama she left was now staring her in the face.

# Chapter 23

When Lyric finally woke up, it didn't take her long to realize that she was still tied up in Russell's hotel room;even the sock in her mouth was still in place. She was sore, hungry and completely dehydrated. Not to mention, her pussy felt like it had been ripped apart. She felt numb, disconnected, humiliated, but most of all dirty and violated. After being betrayed all her life, Lyric never thought in a million years that she would ever be betrayed by Russell; someone she trusted and cared for. *I can't believe Russell would hurt me like this,* Lyric thought. *Even though he always looked at me funny, like he wanted to rape me growing up, I never thought he would actually do it.* She was shocked and knew that damage to their relationship would be irreparable.

*Even though Diesel is a fucking dog and talks a lot of shit to me, he's never hit me. Maybe I'm better off staying with him,* Lyric thought again as tears started to fall down her face.

She struggled and pulled at the tight sheets around her hands trying to get free, but still couldn't manage. She also couldn't bend down to try and untie her feet. However, after wiggling her body toward the edge of the bed, Lyric was able to hop off, but immediately fell to the floor. She felt like screaming, but knew that wouldn't do any good. In her mind, she needed to keep her energy as long as she could.

After several minutes of laying there, Lyric suddenly heard someone knocking on the door. "Housekeeping," a lady said. Lyric immediately started to yell, which sounded more like a moan with the sock stuffed in her mouth. When the lady said, "Housekeeping," one last time and no one answered, she slowly opened the door. Her face was completely alarmed when the Spanish lady found Lyric on the floor. She quickly walked over and untied her.

"Oh, my goodness. Who do this to you? Do need I call police?" the housekeeper asked in her broken English. She helped Lyric back on the bed.

"No, my boyfriend and I were just playing a game," Lyric replied with a forced smile. Lyric had to lie because she didn't want Russell to get in trouble before she got to Diesel's money. "Can you come back later please?" Lyric asked.

"Are you sure?"

When Lyric nodded her head, the housekeeper turned around and left the room.

Lyric's legs felt extremely weak as she stood up and walked into the bathroom. After looking at herself in the mirror, tears began to flow again when she saw the large bruise on her left cheek. "This is a fucking nightmare!" Lyric touched her face gently. 'I need to get out of here before he comes back!"

Lyric quickly made her way back into the room and went straight to the closet. Because Russell had ripped her dress and even her panties, she had to go through his clothes to try and find something to wear. She eventually found an Evisu sweat suit that was too big and threw it on. Something wasn't right with Russell, and she intended on finding out what it was.

Deciding to go through his things, she reached inside a black bookbag he had hidden in the corner of the closet and pulled out a large vanilla envelope. Lyric hesitated when she read the words *Confidential* on the envelope, but curiosity quickly took over. Inside were Russell's release papers from prison along with several other papers including a copy of the incident report with C.O. Douglas. As she began to read, her eyes became enlarged when she read the section about Russell being sent to the prison's Psychiatric Ward.

"What the fuck?" Lyric said out loud. She fumbled through the rest of the papers and found a medical report from Dr. O'Malley indicating he'd been diagnosed with paranoid schizophrenia and given a prescription for some medicine called Zyprexa. When she reached further in the bag, she saw a notebook that instantly took her back to her childhood. She'd always been curious as to what Russell was writing, and as soon as she opened it, her mouth dropped.

From the very first page to the last, Russell had several pictures of black objects that appeared to be ghosts, blood, demons, knifes, anything that represented evil or death. He also had words or sometimes sentences in the book, which alarmed her even more. Things like:

*Stop the voices from talking in my head!!!

*I want to drug Lyric! Her panties smell like vanilla. I would love to rape her.

*All I need is money and Lyric and the voices will go away.

*Love Lyric for life! I will always protect her!

*Lyric, Lyric, Lyric Lyric, and Russell forever.

*I hate my wife. Killing her. Fun.

*I hate my mother. I wish I'd killed her.

*Why do I keep hearing voices? They won't stop!!!

*I don't need medicine.

*Liyah is a dumb bitch. Pam is a dumb bitch. I hate them all.

*Diesel must die!!! He will never have Lyric!!!

"Russell is a fucking lunatic," Lyric said. She quickly put the papers back inside the envelope and placed the notebook back where she found it. "I gotta get the fuck outta here." She looked at the clock beside the bed that read 9:00 a.m. She had no idea where Russell was or when he was coming back.

After grabbing her shoes, Lyric walked over to the couch. She also looked for her phone, but couldn't find it. She needed to call Diesel to see where he was. "Shit, Russell must have my phone."

Lyric walked over to the nightstand where the hotel phone was and realized that it was gone as well. Russell's crazy-ass had obviously taken the phone and ripped the cord out of the wall. When she checked her purse, luckily he hadn't taken her keys.

"Russell got some problems," Lyric said to herself as she left the room and quickly got on the elevator. After successfully getting away in her truck, she headed home to change her clothes and get to a phone. She hoped she was able to get to Diesel before Russell did. Even though she wanted Diesel's money, killing him was never a part of the plan.

Lyric drove home looking in the rear view mirror constantly. Russell had her paranoid and completely on edge. As she continued to drive, thoughts of what he might do to Diesel after what he'd done to her began to dance around in her head. Suddenly, Lyric heard the sound of a loud horn beeping from a car that she almost hit while changing lanes.

"Shit!" she yelled, then gripped the wheel. After almost jumping out of her skin, Lyric tried to focus on the road and make it home in one piece. When she finally pulled up in her driveway a few minutes later, she sighed in relief. Once she pulled into the garage, Lyric pushed the button for the garage to go back down then quickly ran inside and set the alarm.

She took a Tylenol that was in her master bathroom as

soon as she got upstairs. She then grabbed the cordless phone off the charger and called Diesel, but, didn't get an answer. Because Diesel was so secretive with her, Lyric had no idea what time his plane was getting in from Miami. "This is a time when I really need to know where you are!" she began to shout.

After calling Diesel two more times, Lyric took off Russell's sweat suit and jumped in the shower. She could smell his scent all over her body and she scrubbed as hard as she could. It felt like her skin was burning by the time she made it to her legs. Lyric continued to scrub when she heard the house phone ringing. Thinking it might be Diesel, she quickly cut the water off and jumped out the shower.

"Hello, Hello!" Lyric answered as water dripped from her naked body.

"Lyric, where the hell have you been?" Portia asked.

"Oh, hey Portia," Lyric replied in a dry tone.

"Damn, I can tell you wanted somebody else to be on the other end of this phone instead of me."

"I was hoping you were Diesel calling."

"You still sitting around waiting on him to call I see."

"Portia now is not the time for a fucking lecture. I'm about to go take care of something. I'll call you later."

"No wait, have you talked to Russell? He and Sheena got into a fight at the airport about an hour ago. She pissed him off like always and he started choking her. I need to find him before he gets into some more trouble and end up back in prison. I can't let that happen. He is a good man," Portia announced.

"Portia, Russell is far from the fucking Mr. Nice Guy you portray him to be."

"What are you talking about, Lyric? First Sheena, now you?"

"Look, Portia I gotta go."

"I'm on my way over, we need to talk. So stay your ass there until I get there."

Knowing her persistent friend was not going to let up, Lyric agreed. "Hurry up. I have something to do!" CLICK.

At that moment, Lyric started thinking about what Russell had done to her all over again. *If he'd just waited a little longer I might've given him the pussy. Now, I have to decide whether or not I should tell Portia that he raped me.*

Thirty minutes later, Lyric's door bell rung. After peeking out the window, to make sure it wasn't Russell, Lyric opened to the door for Portia and noticed that Sheena and Diva were with her. Both Sheena and Diva didn't look like themselves at all. Both seemed down and out of it. Looking in Sheena's eyes, Lyric could tell she was really upset about something. She then looked at Portia.

"You look nice and rested…and tanned," Lyric mentioned.

"Thanks," Portia replied. "She wanted to tell her friend all about her trip, but knew it wasn't the right time. "I wish I could say the same to you. What happened?" She pointed to Lyric's face. "Don't tell me Diesel hit you?"

Lyric rolled her eyes. "No, he didn't. Look, I don't really wanna talk about that right now."

"Well, have you talked to Russell yet? I called the Holiday Inn, but they said he checked out days ago. Do you know where he might be?" Portia inquired.

"Is that why you came over here, to talk about Russell?" Lyric asked as they all walked into the living room.

"Sort of. I told you over the phone that he and Sheena got into it at the airport, so I need to find him," Portia replied. "I even brought Sheena over here, so we could all talk about it."

Lyric had way more important things to do right now, so she had to hurry the conversation along. She looked at Sheena. "What happened?"

"Russell is Diva's father," Sheena blurted out then lowered her head.

"What?" Both Lyric and Portia said at the same time.

Diva just stared at a picture of Lyric and Diesel inside the built in shelves.

Sheena sighed. "Yeah, he is. Remember years ago when Russell took me to Myrtle Beach for my birthday?" Both Portia and Lyric shook their heads that they remembered. "Well, I told Russell I was pregnant on that trip thinking he would be happy like I was, but I was wrong. He was mad. He completely lost it and flipped out. He hit me in the stomach with several vicious blows causing me to fall to my knees in pain. He then leaped over on top of me punching me repeatedly in the face and stomach. I balled up in the fetal position trying to block his blows until all of a sudden, it was as if something made him stop and he ran out the room. Someone called 911 after hearing my screams." Everyone in the room seemed stunned. As Sheena told the story, Lyric had several flashbacks of Russell attacking her the same way.

"That crazy bastard tried to kill me and my unborn baby. I regret that I never told y'all the truth, but I wanted to forget about it and move on with me life. He never called to check on me or have any remorse for beating my ass. So, since he didn't want to be Diva's father, I chose to not tell anyone he was. I made up the story about the guy in South Carolina. I know it sounds stupid, but at the time I was hurt."

"Wow, I had no idea," Portia said still in shock.

Sheena wanted to get everything off her chest while she was on a roll. "I also never shared with anyone that my father molested me for years." Sheena started to cry. "My father threatened to kill me if I ever told anybody. And y'all remember how big and strong my father was. I was scared as shit of that man. Eventually, I just blocked all that shit out and tried to live a normal life. But I was headed for destruction the way I was running the streets."

Portia and Lyric were completely surprised. Now, it all made since as to why Sheena was so wild and didn't go to her father's funeral. Sheena turned to Diva. "I've been a horrible mother to you over the years, but if you forgive me, I promise to do better. I know I have to gain your trust and hell, even change my lifestyle, but I'll do whatever it takes to start over with you." Mother, daughter time was something they never experienced.

Diva was floored. She'd never heard her mother so sincere in her entire life. It felt good to hear her say all the right things for once. She started crying as well, then went to hug her mother. "I would love that."

After hearing Sheena's confession, Lyric decided not to even tell what had happened to her. She wanted to handle Russell's ass herself, but she at least had to tell her what she'd found at the hotel.

"Portia your cousin is sick, and when I say that, I mean it literally. I found some of his paperwork from jail and it stated that Russell was admitted to the psych ward. The doctor in the prison diagnosed him with paranoid schizophrenia. I saw a prescription for some type of medicine that he was on in there." Everyone seemed stunned as Lyric continued. "He killed his wife on purpose. It wasn't an accident. He wrote it down in one of those notebooks he always carries around."

Portia placed her hand over her mouth. "My grandmother always told me that she thought something was wrong with him. I kinda knew it too, but I just ignored it. I never thought it was that bad." At that moment, Portia excused herself from the room.

"Are you and Diva going to be okay?" Lyric asked Sheena.

"Yes, we're gonna be fine. It's funny how it took Russell's crazy-ass to make us closer though. Thank you for always picking up my slack and being there for her when I was out in the streets," Sheena stated. "It feels good to be able to face all this shit and get it off my chest. I even asked your cousin Kendra to leave because I was living a lie. I love men, and the only reason I was with women was because I was confused."

"Auntie Lyric, can I go get something to drink?" Diva asked.

Lyric frowned. "Since when do you have to ask me

something like that? Of course." As Diva left the room, Lyric looked back at her friend and spoke in a low tone. "I'm glad to hear about Kendra, but I also wanted to tell you not to worry about Russell. Don't worry. He'll get his."

Sheena knew that look in Lyric's eye. She was up to something and she wanted in. "Just be careful because that fool is crazy."

"Trust me. I know," Lyric said, hugging Sheena.

At that moment, Sheena knew she had one more thing to confess. She looked at Lyric directly in the eyes and just blurted it out. "I slept with Diesel after Portia's bachlorette party."

Lyric eyes became two sizes their normal size. "What?"

Sheena lowered her head. "I went back to my job after Portia put me out that night, and apparently I saw Diesel there. I didn't remember much, but he told me that I was going off on him about that other girl. Then apparently all that changed once I started drinking. The next morning when I woke up, he was in my bathroom."

Lyric went off. "How could you? Why didn't you tell me?"

Sheena wiped away a few tears. "I'm sorry. I never meant to hurt you, Lyric. I would've never done anything like that. I guess I just had too much to drink."

"I can't believe this. How could you stoop so fucking low, Sheena? Were you that jealous of me? Did you have to go and fuck my man? How much money did you ask him for?"

Diva came back into the room, as Sheena continued to plead her case. "Auntie Lyric, don't be mad. My mother was going to tell you. I even saw them in the room and I was going to tell you, but Diesel threatened to kill us." It wasn't exactly what Diesel said, but it was close enough. For once, Diva had to vouch for her mother.

Seeing how sincere Diva was, put Lyric at ease a bit. She knew her and Sheena's relationship would never be the same after this, and decided to just let it go. Besides, what's done was done. They'd already fucked, so nothing that she did or said was going to change that.

Sheena hugged Lyric again. "Please forgive me. I'm so sorry. I promise to change my ways." It wasn't long before Diva joined in.

Portia came back into the room and quickly joined in as well. "Group hug," she suggested. "Sheena, I'm so sorry for what Russell did to you."

Sheena forced a smile. "It's not your fault that you have a special cousin."

Everyone including Lyric started laughing.

"Are y'all ready to go? I have to go to a dinner party with Charles and some of his colleagues in less then three hours," Portia stated to Sheena and Diva. She then turned to Lyric. "I'll call you later." When Portia turned around to leave, she suddenly stopped. "Oh, by the way…since we're all confessing about shit. I found out on my honeymoon that Charles may want to be a damn cross dresser." Everyone in the room had their mouth hanging open, and didn't say a word. "But don't worry. I can handle his ass."

As Sheena walked out the door, she really wanted to stay and see what Lyric had planned for Russell, hell she even wanted to be involved, but knew it was best for once to stay drama free.

# Chapter 24

Russell sat crouched down, dressed in all black, in Ski's freshly bought black Lincoln Navigator he'd just purchased with Remo's money. Russell had gone by Ski's apartment and switched cars thinking his rental was hot at the moment. He was backed up in a dark wooded area across the street from Diesels stash house. The street was damn near dark being that it was only two street lights that existed on the whole block. He'd been watching the house now for hours, and couldn't wait until he saw something.

Russell was a bit skeptical about doing the heist due to the fact that he was going on Lyric's word that this was where Diesel's money was and hadn't had a chance to do his normal research. Normally before a heist, he would immediately get on the niggas trail. Follow him, clocking his every move until the victim lead him straight to the money. However, he just had to take her word on this one. Little did Lyric know, as much as Russell loved her, he would've done this one for free.

"I hope Lyric is okay. I've been gone since this morning," Russell said. In his mind, he just knew she was still tied up in his hotel room. "I lost it when I thought about her giving the pussy to everybody but me." He smiled when he thought about the four thousand dollar David Yurman black onyx and diamond bracelet he'd purchased from Neiman Marcus. "I know she won't be mad that I forced myself on her after I put that on her arm. Shit, I could tell by the look in her eyes she wanted me anyway."

He sat watching for any activity for the next three hours as he carried on a conversation with his dead grandmother about the weather. He peeped up when he saw a grey F350 Dully truck with 26'inch wheels pull up. "I wonder who that is."

The truck pulled up in front of the house and Russell watched as a tall slender man got out and went to the back bed of the truck. All he saw was the guy's iced out jewels gleaming in the dull light. Moments later, the guy started unloading boxes then carried them inside the stash house.

When Russell saw him go inside, his robbing skills instantly kicked in as he grabbed his black duffle bag and jumped out the truck. Russell's previous experiences in this situation were to quickly sneak his victim when they arrived at home. Most of the time their hands were full, giving them no time to gather their thoughts.

Russell quietly eased up beside the Ford, then stooped down. Russell paused when he heard the guy come back outside, talking on the phone. The bed of the truck was still open, letting Russell know the guy was coming back out to retrieve something. He listened as the dude had a loud conversation with a female on speaker phone.

"I told you, I just got back in town, Ma. I'll swing through in a little while. Lyric don't know I'm back yet, so I need to go put out a fire wit' her ass first. I can't wait to get rid of her. She a fuckin' pain in my ass. At least you don't' nag the fuck out of me like she does."

"Diesel, you know I'm a better woman than she is. I hope you know that bitch Sasha is going around telling everybody you have twins with her. Is that true, baby?"

"Mannn, I'm gettin' real tired of that bitch tellin' lies, real talk. She went by the house and told Lyric that same shit. Now I have to deal wit' her needy-ass actin' all crazy when I get home. If I didn't have to come back and handle this business, I would've stayed my ass in Miami for awhile. Fuck this shit!"

"Damn, baby it's like that? Well, as long as you fly me out there with you when you go back, I'm cool," the female replied.

As Russell listened to the conversation, the angrier he became. The only thing he was happy about was the fact that the person in the truck was indeed Diesel. It must've been his lucky day. Russell just knew he would have to stake out the house for at least two days before Diesel showed up. *I'm going to get this nigga*, Russell thought then began hitting himself in the head repeatedly with his hands. He was in rage.

"Let me go baby, this is my man Jabari on the other end. Get that pussy ready, I'll be over there in a few."

"Okay baby, I'll be waiting."

"What up boy?" Diesel said clicking over to the other line.

"I need to holla at you about something when you get back in town," Jabari announced.

"I'm back now. Damn nigga you alright, the shit sound urgent."

"It's not urgent. I just need to talk to you."

"Well, I'll come by in the mornin'. I gotta go handle that dumb shit wit' Lyric right now. You sure you alright, nigga? Is it about a bitch? I told you to stop fallin' in love with these broads. All they see is dollar signs. Plus, we need to discuss Miami."

"I'll see you in the mornin'," Jabari said and hung up.

Diesel placed his phone in his pocket and walked back to the truck and grabbed a few more boxes. Russell instantly recognized the name Jabari from the phone call and hoped he wasn't planning to tell Diesel about him sleeping with Lyric and giving up the stash spot location. If so, he needed to get Diesel's ass right now.

Russell checked the block to make sure no one was coming or noticed him hiding on the side of Diesel's truck. He waited for Diesel to walk to the back of the truck to get some more boxes so he could catch him off guard. As soon as he heard Diesel coming, Russell was ready.

"Get your fucking hands up!" Russell ordered in a demanding tone.

When Diesel looked up, Russell had the same Glock Ski had given him from the last robbery pointed directly at his head. "Yo' what the fuck you doin' son?" Diesel asked trying to keep his composure.

"Where's the money at?" Russell asked, pushing the gun further into his head.

"All I have is my jewelry. You can take all this shit, its worth a lot,"
Diesel said removing it.

"I don't want that shit," Russell announced. "Let's go." Russell forced Diesel into the house then closed and locked the door. Seconds later, he bashed Diesel in the head with the butt of the gun and knocked him onto the dusty floor. Blood splattered down Diesel's face instantly.

"I already know you got money up in here, so get your bitch-ass up and get it."
Russell scanned the dirty stash house.

It was a dingy green leather couch and 56'inch big screen sitting in the living room. A cheap, glass top dining room table with black iron chairs was sitting in the small kitchen area. He could see in both of the bedrooms. One had just a mattress on the floor and the other had what looked like a queen sized bed in it. Why there were any beds in the house to begin with, Russell had no idea.

"Yo', you wastin' yo' time, son. I don't have any money here. This is just the spot where I bring my other women. I have a wifey and two daughters, so I try to keep shit away from home," Diesel tried to convince.

"Nigga, don't nobody want to hear all that bullshit. I know you got a girl who you treat like shit," Russell said, waving the gun around. "Let's go check these other rooms. I know its some money in here, I can smell it!"

Diesel got up wondering if the nigga really knew his girl or if he was just trying to get in his head. "You can search all day. Its no money in this house. You might as well kill me!" Diesel yelled, trying to see if the nigga was a real killer or all talk.

Russell punched Diesel in the stomach so hard he threw up the food he'd just eaten. "Shut the fuck up you lying mutha-fucka!" Russell shouted as he grabbed one of the dining room chairs, his duffel bag, then pushed Diesel in the bedroom.

"I told you I didn't have shit in here, nigga," Diesel said, knowing this situation wasn't good.

Tired of his mouth, Russell pushed Diesel into the chair then hit him in the back of neck with the gun before tying him up. Diesel was out cold immediately.

Hours later, Diesel finally came to. He tried to move his hands hoping he could loosen the tight ropes that held him to a chair inside the deserted bedroom, but couldn't. Diesel just needed to get loose and over to the other bedroom where he had his guns stashed in the closet. His entire body was numb and his face was burning. The blood that once ran down his face was now dried up and covered most of his shirt.

*Who is that crazy mutherfucka tryna rob me? Is he some of Sasha's people*, Diesel wondered. He had no idea who Russell was. *I ain't never seen that nigga around town.*

Diesel knew he'd fucked over a lot of people in his day so it could've been any number of people. But he knew if he got free, he would surely kill him. He tugged at the ropes again, but they were just too tight, almost as if a fucking boy scout had tied them. He looked around at the ransacked house. He then looked in the direction of where his money was hidden and was re-lieved that it hadn't been detected.

Diesel wondered what time it was. He knew that the

nosey neighbor, Mrs. Jackson, left for her volunteer job every morning at 6:00 a.m. like clockwork. He licked on a small piece of the tape across his mouth trying to loosen it so he could yell for help as soon as he heard her dogs barking. They normally barked as soon as she walked out and headed to her raggedy mini van. He was able to loosen it some and mumbled loudly, hoping some one could hear him, but seriously doubted it.

Suddenly, Diesel heard footsteps coming in his direction, realizing that Russell was still in the house.

Russell reached in Diesel's pocket and pulled out his cell phone. "I heard you mumbling in here. Do that shit again and see if I don't take your life right now," Russell threatened.

He paced back and forth with two guns pointed in Diesel's direction. Diesel immediately recognized his .357 Sig Sauer and knew Russell had found his gun collection stashed inside the closet wall.

Russell repeatedly hit himself in the head with the gun saying, "Stop talking to me, stop talking to me! Now is not a good time."

Diesel watched as Russell carried on a whole conversation with himself.

*Yo, this nigga is not playin' wit' a full deck. Damn, I might not make it outta here alive,* Diesel thought. *I shoulda told Jabari to meet me over here when he wanted to talk.*

His mind quickly switched to Lyric and how he might not see her beautiful face again and wished he hadn't hurt her so many times. *She's is my ride or die chick and been by my side from day one.* Diesel made himself a promise that if he did make it out alive he would marry Lyric and do right by her, make some pretty babies and enjoy life. He'd totally forgotten that Lyric told me that she couldn't even have children.

Diesel looked Russell up and down trying to figure out where he knew him from. He didn't seem like he was from any of the hoods Diesel hustled at. "I never forget a face and in the four years I've been in Charlotte, I've never seen this nigga before. Maybe he's one of the nigga's I did dirty in New York. I knew my grimy past would catch up with me sooner or later," Diesel said to himself.

Russell walked toward Diesel and leaned over, getting in his face. "I'm gonna ask your bitch-ass one more time. Where's the money? I tore this crib up. I know it's here, I can feel it."

"I don't have any money!"

At that moment, there was a loud shot, and Diesel instantly yelled out in pain. Russell had shot him in the left leg.

"Now, do you wanna tell me where it is?" Russell asked.

When Diesel didn't respond, Russell grabbed the duct tape off the table and tightly wrapped it around Diesel's mouth, nose then his entire face. By the way Diesel squirmed, Russell could tell he was having trouble breathing. Diesel gasped for air.

"I'm gonna give you a little more time to see if your ass knows where the money is. But you better know by the time I get back or else," Russell said, slamming the door.

# LOVE HEIST

# Chapter 25

Russell left Diesel at the stash house before he flipped out and killed him, which would've been way too soon. Especially since he still didn't have what he came for in the first place. He knew the money was somewhere inside that house and planned to find it even if he had to tear down the damn walls with his bare hands. He didn't want to tell Lyric that he had Diesel yet. He wanted to get the money first and surprise her. In his mind, if he did it that way, Lyric would be happy that he kept his word and would forgive him for raping her.

"Which it really wasn't a rape, just good old rough sex. The pussy is mine, been mine since day one. She just didn't want to admit it," Russell said out loud. "She better like my gift. She puts up with Diesel's shit and forgives him after he buys her things, so why not me?"

He pulled into a drive-thru a few minutes later, to get Lyric something to eat. He knew she was starving and probably dying of thirst.

"Welcome to Burger King. Would you like to try a value meal?" the lady through the speaker asked.

"Yeah, let me get some of those French Toast Sticks and some hashbrowns," Russell replied.

"I'm sorry sir, but breakfast was over at 10:30. We're

only serving lunch now."

Russell wasn't in the mood to comply with that non-sense. "Then why the fuck do y'all have pictures of the breakfast food on the board if people can't get the shit!"

The lady paused. "Sir, the foul language is unnecessary. Now, would you like something from the lunch menu or not?"

"Just give me two chicken sandwiches with cheese, fries and two sweet teas then, damn."

"Sir, we don't have any sweet tea right now."

"Well, just give me two Sprites then, bitch."

The woman paused again "Will that be all, sir?"

"Yeah, that's it." He had no idea that a bunch of spit would probably be on his sandwiches.

Russell was heated. "I hate buying this fast food bullshit. If I had an oven in my room I would cook Lyric a nice gourmet meal that she would love. I can't wait until we're man and wife. I plan to cook for her all the time and serve her breakfast in bed on a regular. I bet that nigga Diesel can't top that!"

When Russell pulled up to pay for the food, he felt Lyric's phone vibrating in his pocket. It was a text message from Sheena.

**Lyric I just want to say sorry once again. I hope u find it in your heart to forgive me. Thanks for listening to me about Russell. It's good to finally get everything off my chest. Call me if u wanna talk. Sheena**

"I know Sheena told Lyric about the episode at the airport and Diva being my daughter. I'm sick of that bitch, not only did she disobey me years ago and get pregnant, but she had the baby and kept it a damn secret from everybody for sixteen years. I'm going to get her ass once and for all as soon as I take care of Diesel."

After getting his food from the woman at the window, who threw Russell his food, he headed toward the hotel. He hoped Lyric was in the mood to fuck and wanted to give him some pussy voluntarily. He was horny as hell and would take it again if he had to. Sex with Lyric was the best he ever had in his life, and Russell had sampled a lot of pussy in his days.

He'd stopped by the corner store that sold fresh cut flowers to buy Lyric a dozen of roses. He also grabbed a bottle of wine, cups and some candles. Even though he only had Chicken sandwiches he planned to make it a special candlelit meal.

While driving, his own phone rang and he looked at the caller ID, it was Portia. After calling her number for sixteen years while he was locked up, he knew her number by heart, but Russell wondered how she got his number. He didn't have a chance to give it to her yet.

"What's up cuz," he said, answering the phone.

"Russell, I've been blowing your damn phone up for a while. Come over to my house right now!" Portia demanded.

"Why? How did you get my number anyway?"

"Lyric gave it to me," Portia answered.

Russell frowned. *How the fuck did Lyric give it to her?* He then gave the situation the benefit of the doubt. *Maybe Lyric gave it to Portia while she was in Hawaii.* "Oh, well what's going on?"

"Look, what I just found out about you is disturbing. How could you do that to Sheena?"

"Because she deserved it. I haven't known all this time that I had a daughter, and it's fucked up. Sheena has ruined her!" Russell had promised his self years ago that if he ever had kids he would be in their life and protect them. But how could he protect Diva now after what had taken place between them. How could she ever look at him again without thinking about that night in his car?

"So, Sheena deserved to be beaten while she was pregnant? Even worse, did your wife deserve to die?" Russell wondered again how Portia had gotten her information. "We need to sit down and talk about this."

"I don't have to do shit. What the fuck are you talking about? I didn't kill anybody!"

"Russell don't you dare sit here and lie to me. You can't

go around hurting people and thinking the shit is cool," Portia replied.

For the first time, Russell went off on Portia. "I can do whatever I want. You don't know what I've been through all these years. You have no idea. Don't you ever tell me what to do!"

Portia had never witnessed Russell like this. "You obviously need some help. Why don't you come over here so we can talk?"

"No, I got some better shit to do right now."

Portia was already frustrated. "You know Charles was right about you. If I continue to deal with you, you're gonna be nothing but trouble."

It hurt Russell to hear that, but instead of him understanding, he did what he always does. He snapped. "You know what, fuck you and your husband. I don't like that whack-ass nigga anyway. I can't believe you would side with that nigga over me…over family!" Russell continued to be irate. "Don't you ever call me with this shit again. I'll kill you!" Russell warned before hanging up.

He continued to curse as if he was still on the phone until he pulled in the hotel parking lot. After grabbing all his goodies for Lyric, Russell got out and headed toward the front on a mission. When he got off the elevator, he noticed that his room door was open. He also noticed the big housekeeping cart, which sent him into panic mode.

As soon as he entered the room, he went straight to the bathroom after realizing Lyric was no longer on the bed. "Where's the girl who was in this room?" he asked the Spanish woman.

"Oh, the lady. She lay on the floor when I come in. I untied her," the woman replied. "She not here now."

Russell balled up his fist and went to hit the woman, but changed his mind. He knew she would only go right downstairs and tell someone. "Get your non-talking ass out my damn room!" he yelled. "Clean this shit later!" When the woman walked out, Russell threw the food, flowers and gift up against the wall. He then picked up the mattress off the bed then threw that across the room along with two lamps.

He ran to the closet and grabbed his bag. His hands shook as he pulled out his notebook and started scribbling things in it. When that didn't calm him down, he jumped up and started pacing the floor. The room started spinning and he felt and anxiety attack coming on.

He then saw the vision of his Mama Moses appear on the hotel wall. He heard her voice call out to him. *Russell Arnell King, what have you done? I've always taught you, Portia and Lyric, that family comes first, and look what you've done. Had sex with your own daughter, raped Lyric, and threatened Portia who's like your sister. I'm so ashamed of you!*

Russell immediately dropped to his knees and cried like a baby. He knew he had to get back over to the stash house to find that money. It was the only way Russell knew he could make things right with Lyric.

# Chapter 26

When Lyric pulled up to Diesel's stash spot, she circled the block several times making sure Russell's rental car wasn't parked anywhere in the neighborhood. She'd searched her house before leaving for at least one of Diesel's guns in case she ran into Russell, but came up empty.

"He must've gotten rid of them ever since the night he woke up and I had his
.9 mm pointed to his head for cheating on me again," Lyric said out loud. "Oh, well I'll just have to use my razor and slit Russell's throat if he come my way again. That shit he pulled before is not gonna go down. He'll have to kill me first."

After circling one last time, Lyric parked two blocks over and jumped out her truck dressed in a black hooded sweat suit and black air force ones. She pulled the hood over her head and walked toward the house making sure to constantly check her surroundings.

While searching for Diesel's guns, Lyric found a set of keys that she didn't recognize and prayed that one of them was the key to the stash house. "If not, I'll just break the fucking window out," she said, arriving at the house.

She decided to go around back. After almost tripping over an old lawn mower, Lyric peeped inside the dirty window and saw the television in the living room playing an old, *Good Times* rerun. She tried the first three sets of keys in the back door, but they didn't work.

"Come on…come on," Lyric repeated as she tried the last key. She felt like she'd won the lottery as the key slid into the lock with ease. Turning the knob, Lyric looked behind her to see if anyone was coming before slowly stepping inside.

Other than hearing JJ's character yell, "Dynomite," and the studio audience laughing, the house was extremely quiet. Lyric eased through the kitchen into the living room and down the hall taking small steps. She even tiptoed a few times. Seconds later, Lyric looked into the first bedroom with a dirty mattress on the floor realizing it was empty. When she approached the second bedroom, the door was closed. Lyric stood outside in the hallway for almost two minutes trying to find the courage to open it.

*What if Russell's crazy-ass is hiding on the other side of this door? I can't put nothing past his ass anymore. But I'm here now, so fuck it. I need to try and find Diesel to see if he's hurt. Hell, to see if he's still alive.*

Realizing she was wasting too much time, Lyric turned the knob and slowly peeped inside the room. Her eyes widened when she saw Diesel tied up and badly beaten in the corner of the room. He raised his head when Lyric took off her hood and said his name. He began to mumble something, which Lyric couldn't understand with the duct tape all over his face and mouth. Thinking about her own recent nightmare, Lyric quickly ran over to Diesel and removed all the tape.

"Lyric? Oh, my God baby please come and untie me quick before that fuckin' maniac comes back. He tried to find my money, but he didn't find it," Diesel announced after taking a deep breath.

Suddenly, the business that Lyric really needed to get down to flashed through her mind. "Where is the money?" she asked in a low tone.

For the first time in his life, Diesel didn't have any issues with trust. He pointed to the low ceiling above them. "All my money is up there. You see the air vent. Well, look beside it. There's a big spot that looks like wet paint. All you have to do is get somethin' to knock through that spot, and you'll find the bag." Lyric paused when he mentioned the money "Come on, why the fuck you just standin' there? Untie me!"

Despite all Diesel's wrongdoings, Lyric didn't want to see him dead, so she walked over to the chair. *I'll just have to figure out how to get the money later*. Just as she was about to untie him, Lyric heard the front door open and close.

"Somebody's coming," Lyric whispered.

"Run and hide under the bed, and don't make a sound. This nigga is psycho," Diesel replied. "I'll tell you when it's safe to come out."

Lyric slid on the floor and hid under the bed inside the room. At the moment, as crazy as it was, she began to wonder how many women Diesel had fucked on that very bed. *Why the fuck would he need a bed at a stash house*? Snapping back to reality, Lyric listened as Russell came in the room cussing and yelling at Diesel.

"You ready to come clean and tell me where you hid that money, yet?" Russell asked, waving his gun around. He was so out of it from not being able to find Lyric that he didn't even notice Diesel was no longer taped up.

"I told you before. I don't have any money. All my dough is tied up in a Miami deal, real talk." Diesel said in a low voice.

"Fucking liar!" Russell yelled. He leaned down, spitting in Diesel's face.

"Come on man, shit! I already told you, ain't nothin' here. You might as well let me go," Diesel pleaded.

"Do you think I'm gonna leave this muthafucka empty handed? I don't think so. My girl would kill me anyway. I gotta come back with the loot. I don't have a choice." Russell paused for a minute. "Actually, you taking too damn long. I gotta go find my girl, so you need to hurry the fuck up."

Suddenly, Lyric heard what sounded like the front door being kicked in, which instantly made her jump.

"Who's that, your people?" Russell asked. It wasn't long before Russell cocked his gun like he was ready for war. A short time later, another person came in and gun shots instantly filled the room. From that moment on, it was complete chaos.

"What the fuck? Y'all trying to take me out?" Lyric heard Russell yell.

Lyric slid further under the bed trembling when she heard gunshots again, then a large thump hit the floor. It was definitely a body. Covering her mouth, Lyric laid completely still when she heard footsteps walking around on the old hard wood floors. Lyric prayed who ever it was, didn't flip the mattress over and find her curled up underneath it.

"Your wife was my sister. You killed my sister. She didn't deserve to die," a female voice spoke.

Lyric tried her best to distinguish the voice, but it sounded foreign. She wondered who the girl was talking to.

"I've been waiting sixteen years to get my revenge," the female continued. "Did you really think they were going to let your crazy-ass out if it wasn't for me? I deliberately applied for that job at the prison once I found out where you were. I had dirt on someone on the parole board, and that's how you got approved to be released in the first place. I'd planned to kill your ass in prison with an overdose, but with the investigation on C.O. Douglas, it was too hot to take you out there. That's when I paid Liyah a nice amount for her help." Dr. O'Malley looked over at Liyah who looked beyond frightened. Her hands shook as she held up the .32 caliber pistol.

Dr. O'Malley began to circle Russell whose wounds were bleeding profusely. "Liyah overlooked the fight with you and Big Country on purpose you know. It was all planned. She was supposed to seduce you, then keep you at her house when you got out, but you went psycho on her ass and left town before I could get to you. In the end, she was more than happy to continue working with me after you did that shit to her. So, we tracked your ass down in Charlotte. It was a little difficult to find you at first, but once we did, we've been watching you ever since."

"Yeah, I killed your sister. She was a cheating bitch," Russell said, breathing heavy.

Suddenly, Lyric heard another shot, which immediately put her in panic mode. She could no longer hear Russell and hadn't heard Diesel say a word.

"Let's get the fuck outta here. Someone probably heard all the gunshots," Liyah frantically said.

When she heard the front door close a few seconds later and a car skid away, she quickly came from underneath the bed. He knees became weak instantly when she saw Diesel slumped over in the chair and Russell lying on the floor. Diesel was dead; Russell was barely alive. Lyric could tell that he couldn't breathe by the way he gasped for air.

Running over to Diesel, Lyric instantly checked his pulse, but knew it wouldn't matter. From all the blood covering his chest and neck area, she knew he was gone. Lyric lowered her head. This madness was all her fault. Looking over at Russell, Lyric was about to go over to him, but suddenly stopped. It might've not been the best decision, but she decided to leave him there. In her mind, removing Russell from society forever was probably not a bad thing. At least he couldn't hurt anyone else, which was worth way more than his life.

Lyric kissed her hand, then placed it on Diesel's forehead before going to grab a chair. Moments later, she came back with a hammer. She knew she had to hurry up just in case someone did hear the shots. After finding the spot Diesel told her about, Lyric stood on the chair, then began to hit the ceiling with all her might. She sneezed several times from the dust and dirt that fell.

After getting a nice sized hole, Lyric reached her hand inside, feeling around for the money. At the same time, she glanced at all the bullets holes in the ceiling and walls. It was definitely something out of a Western movie.

When Lyric finally felt the huge bag she struggled to pull

it down, but managed to succeed after several tries. She dragged the duffel bag full of money to the door and looked back over her shoulder one last time. When she did, it was then Lyric noticed Russell staring directly at her. She could see the hurt in Russell's eyes that she was walking out the door with the money and leaving him for dead.

"You should've never crossed me Russell, I trusted you," Lyric said before walking out the house. After finally pulling off, Lyric began to smile. "There's no turning back now."

# Epilogue

## Six months later...

Lyric walked down Melrose Avenue trying to find a new space for her boutique since the place she previously looked at months ago was no longer available. Lyric wished she would've signed the lease, so she didn't have to start all over. The name brand stores that occupied the popular street were just the type of vibe she was looking for in her boutique. It had to be stylish and trendy just like her. The sunny weather, palm trees, nice atmosphere and people with money was right up Lyric's alley. She loved L.A, and wished she'd made the decision to move years ago.

After safely making the forty-six hour drive to L.A with the eight hundred thousand dollars stashed in her truck, Lyric checked into the Beverly Hills Hotel on Sunset Boulevard. A flawless hotel which was just what Lyric needed to get herself together and start her new life. After her short stay in the hotel, she finally purchased an urban-style loft home in a quiet neighborhood called Santee Village. A perfect spot with a gorgeous view for her and the new Maltese puppy she'd purchased to keep her company.

Being around friends all her life, Lyric felt lonely and wished Portia, Sheena and Diva could've made the trip on the west coast with her, but knew that wouldn't work, especially after hearing about all the good news. Sheena and Diva had moved to Atlanta and were getting along great. Diva had apparently started dating guys her own age, and Sheena even had a new man in her life; the first man she'd been faithful to. Portia was also happy with a new baby on the way. She was also happy that Charles hadn't put on anymore female clothing.

Lyric even found herself missing Diesel when she would visit certain places in L.A. like Roscoe's Chicken & Waffles and the trendy steakhouse, STK that they used to go to all the time. Although he cheated on her numerous times, they did have some happy moments with each other, which Lyric treasured. Not only that, Diesel did take care of her and gave her any and everything she wanted, and for that...Lyric was grateful. It was too bad the only thing he couldn't give her was faithfulness. However, Lyric was glad to be away from all the drama of Diesel's countless women. She'd heard that there were five women at his funeral fighting when they found out about each other.

When Lyric saw the famous green and white Starbucks sign, she decided to stop in for a frozen strawberry lemonade and a brownie. After retrieving her order, she decided to sit at one of the tables outside and browse though different property listings she'd accumulated throughout the day. It didn't take long for one of the listings that read; Beautiful and Stylish Boutique For Sale to catch her eye. It sounded like the perfect spot.

"Excuse me, isn't your name, Lyric?" a male voice asked, pulling Lyric's attention away from reading. When she looked up it was Maxwell Tyson, the fine ass-lawyer she'd met a while back in Charlotte.

"Yes, hello Maxwell, how are you?" Lyric said, extending her hand.

"I'm impressed that you remember me," he said smiling.

"How could I forget?"

"What are you doing in L.A.?"

"I live here now," Lyric informed.

Maxwell smiled again. "How ironic. I'm moving to L.A. in a few weeks. I just opened up my own law firm here on Wilshire Boulevard." Maxwell looked around like he was searching for someone. "Does your man live out here, too?"

"I don't have a man, not yet anyway," Lyric replied with a huge smile.

"Well, I'll have to see what I can do to help you out. Do you mind if I join you?" Maxwell asked.

"Please do." Lyric replied. She smiled to herself thinking, *maybe true love does exist after all.*

Russell finished up some paper work in his office. He had to make sure all the orders for the next day's menu were in place. He was serving a business party in his cozy and intimate dining room that sat up to thirty people. After powering down his computer, he grabbed his leather jacket. He was exhausted and ready to head to his new condo in Allyson Park in the South Charlotte area. He thought about calling one of his women to meet him there just so he could curl up under a soft body. Ever since Lyric had disappeared with all Diesel's money, he felt hurt and lonely. At least he knew she wasn't with Diesel because his ass was dead. He wondered if he hadn't raped her if they would be together now instead of her leaving him to die at the stash house. Luckily, the nosy neighbor, Mrs. Jackson had called the police once she heard the gunshots allowing them to get to Russell just in time. He just wished they'd gotten there before Lyric got a chance to leave. Even though he was unresponsive and had a weak pulse, once he arrived at the hospital, he still managed to survive the gunshot wounds to his chest and abdomen.

"The only woman I wanted to share my life with was

Lyric, but she fucking left me. The story of my life," Russell said out loud.

Since he'd opened up his restaurant, consuming himself with his love for cooking, the hallucinating and voices seem to ease up…some. The medicine he made himself take everyday helped out tremendously.

Russell walked to the front of his restaurant called, *The Best Kept Secret.* The 3,000 square foot space was soft and warm with beautifully decorated deep emerald colored walls with flat screen televisions in each corner. The soaring ceilings, candle lit tables, thick white linen tablecloths, and polished wooden floors offered a stunning atmosphere which couldn't be found anywhere else in the local area. Not to mention, the beautiful view over looking the city was breathtaking. Russell's menu featured innovative cuisine as well as his mostly requested contemporary southern-fried chicken with a side of mac n' cheese, or sautéed red snapper and garlic grilled shrimp. Even his phenomenal filet mignon cooked to 1600 degrees of perfection was to die for.

Russell had planned to enroll in The International Culinary School of Art to follow his passion and explore more creativity toward his cooking skills as soon as he got the chance. He also wanted to hire some well rounded top chefs. For now, he had to deal with Ski, who constantly fucked up the food orders. Russell knew as soon as the business picked up, he was firing Ski's ass.

He grabbed his keys, clicked off all the lights and set the alarm before unlocking the front door with a huge smile. Russell couldn't wait to add the new chicken and sausage gumbo to the menu. However, that smile instantly faded when he felt a gun being pushed in his back. That's when he heard the shot… two of them actually.

Russell felt his body fall to the ground. He felt pain in his chest as his body temperature dropped. He reached in his pocket to grab his cell phone to call for help, but couldn't reach it. The pain was too bad. Visions of all the people he'd done wrong over his entire life flashed in front of him. All the niggas he'd robbed...all the women he'd beat, raped and deserted. He lifted his head to try and see who'd shot him, but his vision was blurry. He was finally able to see the face when Remo came closer and stood over him with the gun pointed to his head.

"Remember me, nigga? I had a long talk with your boy Ski and after some persuading I got him to give you up. Where's my money nigga?" Russell looked at him but didn't answer. "Did you think, you were gonna roll up in my crib and get away with it? Did you use it to buy this fucking restaurant?" Remo asked. "I see your ass didn't die when those two bitches went to that house and busted you and that other nigga up. But don't worry...I'ma make sure this hit is successful!"

As Russell went to say, *fuck you*, Remo shot off another round. This time it was at point blank range to the head. This time, Russell was finally gone.

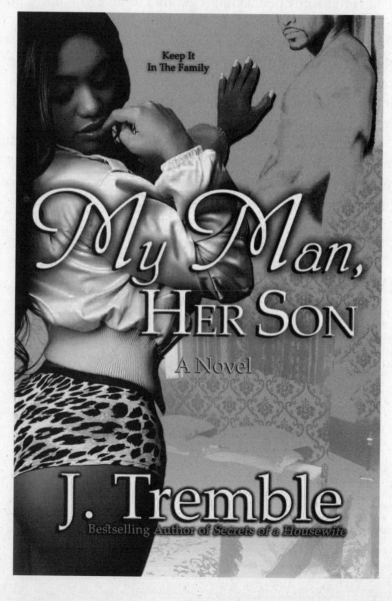

# COMING SOON

A NOVEL BY

# MISS KP

**MAIL TO:**
PO Box 423
Brandywine, MD 20613
301-362-6508

**FAX TO:**
301-856-4116

# ORDER FORM

| | |
|---|---|
| Date: | Phone: |
| Email: | |

Ship to:
Address:
City & State:                    Zip:

*Make all money orders and cashiers checks payable to:* **Life Changing Books**

| Qty. | ISBN | Title | Release Date | Price |
|------|------|-------|--------------|-------|
| | 0-9741394-5-9 | Nothin Personal by Tyrone Wallace | Jul-06 | $ 15.00 |
| | 0-9741394-2-4 | Bruised by Azarel | Jul-05 | $ 15.00 |
| | 0-9741394-7-5 | Bruised 2: The Ultimate Revenge by Azarel | Oct-06 | $ 15.00 |
| | 0-9741394-3-2 | Secrets of a Housewife by J. Tremble | Feb-06 | $ 15.00 |
| | 0-9724003-5-4 | I Shoulda Seen It Comin by Danette Majette | Jan-06 | $ 15.00 |
| | 0-9741394-4-0 | The Take Over by Tonya Ridley | Apr-06 | $ 15.00 |
| | 0-9741394-6-7 | The Millionaire Mistress by Tiphani | Nov-06 | $ 15.00 |
| | 1-934230-99-5 | More Secrets More Lies by J. Tremble | Feb-07 | $ 15.00 |
| | 1-934230-98-7 | Young Assassin by Mike G. | Mar-07 | $ 15.00 |
| | 1-934230-95-2 | A Private Affair by Mike Warren | May-07 | $ 15.00 |
| | 1-934230-94-4 | All That Glitters by Ericka M. Williams | Jul-07 | $ 15.00 |
| | 1-934230-93-6 | Deep by Danette Majette | Jul-07 | $ 15.00 |
| | 1-934230-96-0 | Flexin & Sexin by K'wan, Anna J. & Others | Jun-07 | $ 15.00 |
| | 1-934230-92-8 | Talk of the Town by Tonya Ridley | Jul-07 | $ 15.00 |
| | 1-934230-89-8 | Still a Mistress by Tiphani | Nov-07 | $ 15.00 |
| | 1-934230-91-X | Daddy's House by Azarel | Nov-07 | $ 15.00 |
| | 1-934230-87-1- | Reign of a Hustler by Nissa A. Showell | Jan-08 | $ 15.00 |
| | 1-934230-86-3 | Something He Can Feel by Marissa Montelih | Feb-08 | $ 15.00 |
| | 1-934230-88-X | Naughty Little Angel by J. Tremble | Feb-08 | $ 15.00 |
| | 1-934230847 | In Those Jeans by Chantel Jolie | Jun-08 | $ 15.00 |
| | 1-934230855 | Marked by Capone | Jul-08 | $ 15.00 |
| | 1-934230820 | Rich Girls by Kendall Banks | Oct-08 | $ 15.00 |
| | 1-934230839 | Expensive Taste by Tiphani | Nov-08 | $ 15.00 |
| | 1-934230782 | Brooklyn Brothel by C. Stecko | Jan-09 | $ 15.00 |
| | 1-934230669 | Good Girl Gone bad by Danette Majette | Mar-09 | $ 15.00 |
| | 1-934230804 | From Hood to Hollywood by Sasha Raye | Mar-09 | $ 15.00 |
| | 1-934230707 | Sweet Swagger by Mike Warren | Jun-09 | $ 15.00 |
| | 1-934230677 | Carbon Copy by Azarel | Jul-09 | $ 15.00 |
| | 1-934230723 | Millionaire Mistress 3 by Tiphani | Nov-09 | $ 15.00 |
| | 1-934230715 | A Woman Scorned by Ericka Williams | Nov-09 | $ 15.00 |
| | | | **Total for Books** | $ |
| | | Shipping Charges (add $4.25 for 1-4 books*) | | $ |
| | | **Total Enclosed (add lines)** | | $ |

* Prison Orders- Please allow up to three (3) weeks for delivery.

For credit card orders and orders over 30 books, please contact us at orders@lifechaningbooks.net

*Shipping and Handling of 5-10 books is $6.25, please contact us if your order is more than 10 books.